The Animal Hotel

THE
ANIMAL
HOTEL

BY

Jean Garrigue

NEW YORK

THE EAKINS PRESS

PUBLISHERS

FIRST EDITION

For Josephine Herbst

The Animal Hotel

ONCE a bear kept a small inn for animals. Not many, just a mole or so, a chipmunk, a cat, several birds, a sheep and a deer. Wasps and bees, also inhabitants, didn't count because they were innumerable. All got on pretty well together or the bear wouldn't have had them in the first place for she was a strong character with a proper sense of the fitness of things. If she was going to run a hotel she was going to run it right. She believed in neatness; for her it came before cleanliness. No littered nests for her, with bones on beds and birdseed growing out of chairs. No sir. None of that. Some of the animals grumbled and others sighed at her strong edicts but since the hotel was really very comfortable and quite charming in many ways, they knew they couldn't do better. So they put up with it. The cat stacked his fishheads in a corner and the birds kept their cuttlebones under the bed. Whatever the mole ate he ate all of, so he presented no problem. The deer though the gentlest was the messiest since he left a trail of grasses and half-nibbled shoots and couldn't seem to learn better. The bear often rolled her eyes thinking of that deer: was he really stupid? And yet, so nice! How was it that the nicest were the most stupid? Or was he just stubborn? This neat question often returned to her, and made for a certain moral perplexity. . . .

Things prospered, though. The animals were very good about paying their rent so the bear never had to dun them the first of the month and all pitched in to help her keep things in repair, like proper exits for the mole, in case of necessity, and coverts and brakes for the deer who otherwise might have trampled them down, and warm sunny places for the cat. The chipmunk asked for the least, just a convenient tree to run up, and an old ledge of a wall, preferably abandoned, and in a way he was the tenant the bear liked most. The birds were a nuisance. They had to have chickseed and wouldn't eat wasps of which there was plenitude but had to have special worms brought in and water cress and other seed-bearing grasses the bear hated to bother with. But there it was. She liked them for all their picking and picayune finicking, liked all their clamor at early hours and their general robust cheerfulness.

So the hotel prospered though the bear worked hard, and the animals met at meals or convened in the evenings with the utmost geniality. The birds would sit on the prongs of the deer, the chipmunk would nestle beside the cat while the blind mole would softly sit by himself in a dream of tunnels. None of these animals were married. Perhaps some had been. But it is better not to go into the question of divorce or desertion. Perhaps some wanted to be. It doesn't matter. They were, for our purposes, bachelors, living in single blessedness. And was it so single? Didn't they all meet and chat and share in some way one anothers' lives? Yes they did. The bear saw to that. And saw to more. She hated a mooning self-consciousness, a broodiness that excluded society, she hated the sulks and the pouts (she couldn't bear pouter pigeons), she hated the glooms and the hangdog grief. A sable repentance, like that of the raven, would have finished her off. So if there were broken hearts in her midst, unfulfilled ones, or yearnings for some neat doe, she didn't want to hear of it, least of all did she want any reference to it. Hers was an inn or a hotel, if you will, it wasn't a retreat for the lorn and the lost.

All the animals understood this without its having to be mentioned, for some of them were more subtle than you may think, and especially was the bear, whose past was more complicated than anybody could guess.

So the hotel prospered and acquired a good deal of prestige in the eyes of animals and became famous in its own modest way. When various animals were thinking of retirement it was the hotel they dreamed about. The bear got applications all the time, and often had to stay up late at night pondering over just who should be allowed to come in. She didn't want a crowded place, and the thought of building on, of adding more tunnels and brakes and cubby-holes, filled her with horror. Yet with so many applications filtering in, and some of them quite appealing, quite touching, the bear was hard put to it some nights to know just what she ought to do. She loved her place as it was, she didn't like the thought of expanding, even though it would mean more profits. Did she have any cubs? Who knows, and if she did would she have any idea where they were? So why struggle for the next generation? But still, there was *this* generation, this vixen, newly widowed, and that owl who had lost his hearing, all wanting in, nay, pleading . . . the old, not the new generation knocking at her door!

So like anybody else she had a problem to think about and in the meantime trees fell that the beaver couldn't seem to find time to cut, and besides, he was very expensive, and other bears would get into her private stores of honey, or bribe the bees, maybe, to work for them. There were all these little naggings of life that go with responsibility and sometimes the bear would think: why do I do it, for what am I working my claws off, and sigh in her good coat that would last a lifetime.

But she knew just the same and it didn't take letters of application to tell her. She knew in the evening when her guests gathered round and started to talk or tell tales. How intelligent they were, for all their shortcomings, and how good it made

her feel to watch them tuck in as they did at her fine meals—
and they were fine—didn't the animals constantly tell her so?

In the meantime, though her hotel was secluded, deep as it
was in a woods well manned by foxholes and woodchuck
burrows, by little round black-snake entries, by rabbit warrens
and colonies of the wildest flowers and sentry nests of the owls
and other beasts too dangerous to mention, strangers did pass
it on their way to places where a fine killing had been made and
what sheep's eyes they cast when they saw the spruce dwelling.
There was an outside stairway that no animal would dream to
climb, but there it stood like a little royal honor, and there was
the roof all thatched with hay that the deer in his absentmind-
edness might start to browse on, there it was in its twiggen
rambling, with vines nicely trained round the stairway, for
amongst her other accomplishments, the bear was a great
gardener. And with foxy smile and bleat of praise or a mild
cough these strangers would stop and try to beguile her. Once
an aging hedgehog pretended to fall sick and the bear like a
naive samaritan came out to nurse him. But she had her own
wiles too, maintaining that fresh air was best for him while she
dosed him with French mint tea. So the hedgehog failed in his
ruse. It was the same with the others. The bear was benignant
but mixed with that was a shambling austerity. You couldn't
quite pull the wool over her eyes nor even if you were a good
eater could you get to her heart unless you had other qualities
too, to boot.

There would be musical evenings, for example. What was
the point of being there unless you had a good voice? For the
bear loved quality in a voice, adored resonance, and the bigger
the bray or the bay the better. Even as it was she would sit in
her fur with her blood running cold when an old crow started
to craack! craack! and could be entranced for hours by the
divertimentos of the catbird. Then a change would come upon

her. The animals had all learned to recognize it. A dreaminess, a remoteness, a rumbling there in that great shaggy being. Then it was that the animals wondered what her history had been. . . .

She was a marvelous housekeeper and a marvelous bear but there was a loneliness you noticed in her that you saw in none of the other animals. Even the smug mole who kept to himself so much because he was blind. What you felt was that the mole was solitary because he didn't care and had never known better. The bear seemed to have renounced society.

Now the days were one thing. The animals were off on their own affairs. People like the cat would choose to sit in the hotel and stare out with eyes big as gooseberries at butterflies going by or get excited over a crows' convention or by the sun glinting on a rosebush in the wind. But when the cat was in a mood for excitement, it didn't take a crow—any wasp would do. The deer would crash around in the woods, getting his antlers mixed up with wild grapevine or honeysuckle, and the sheep would butt at a tree to keep in practice. The birds chattered so much that nobody knew what they did. But at night, after supper, all would get together, even the mole, for the evening conversation. The bear set much store by this and just as she loved a good singer, wouldn't have an animal unless he could talk well. She despised to be bored. Everybody had to be able to make up stories or to have suffered or led an adventurous life. Naturally the animals liked to talk about food the way human beings like to talk about money, but the bear said since we eat it and have plenty of it, why go on about it? So the animals had to be very inventive and sheep vied with mole in recalling nanny's stories about milch cows and grubs. Then it was also that the animals vied with one another to see who could get into her lap and stay longest. Really, they seemed to think she was made for clambering over while the bear as they did it affected a sternness she couldn't possibly feel and sometimes had to break out laughing at her own little imposture while she pretended, of course, that they were tickling her. Sometimes there were almost quarrels so the bear taught them to take turns. One night it would be the deer's time to rest his great chin on her shoulder, and what positive bliss he would be in until the bear, who didn't like to hurt anybody's feelings, would have to invent an excuse for getting up. His chin was so heavy with all those antlers above! The sheep adored to sit on her hind legs with her forefeet in the bear's lap while bear would smooth burrs out of her side wool or beggar's ticks from a tassel. The sheep's eyes always lost their hard-boiled look when she was like that. As for chipmunk and cat, they would nuzzle and snuggle, fur on fur, as if she were their own mother.

After this cosy interlude the bear would say: time for bed! and off the animals would go, some to a turf cushion (out of respect for the goose none of the cushions were stuffed with feathers) and others to fresh hay bolsters. On rainy nights the cat would stay in; otherwise he would be out till one or two in the morning. And though he did come in silently he was often noisy about getting into bed and would frequently awake the bear who would moan out in great distress Oh! Oh! for she would have been startled from a dream. Was she unearthing a pot of honey or seeing it snatched from her? The bear was not one of those who sit around the breakfast table talking of that submerged life one lives in sleep. Let the cat mew on of his pedestrian encounters with cows and horses, let the mole coarsely refer to dead birds he had stumbled across in his underground chambers, and the deer speak of that fawn he might have fathered, with such charming buds of horns, one at each temple, but with the legs, oh horrors, of a goat! The bear kept her counsel, rolling her head slightly, and yet they all knew she dreamed, so wakeful she was, and such a slight sleeper. Did she but know it, the pride of her silence was making her the "heroine of a thousand anecdotes."

Now the bear was quite handsome in her own fashion, with a good short muzzle and thrilling white teeth. Her coat was always well groomed and nicely perfumed, smelling of beeswax mixed with pomade that the deer applied twice a week or so and her paws were quite delicate considering her size. As for her claws, they were always most polished and trimmed. When she walked it was with a springing gait, quite lightly for one of such poundage, an almost musical gait as if she might have gone sometime to sea. Only when she was very tired or distracted would she resort to that lolloping and head-rolling lumber that most bears are prone to employ, and even so, when she did it was with her own distinction. Needless to say, she was never to be caught in a pompous waddling like an old drake or a gluttonous goose. There was one curiosity, however, in all her get-up. Most bears have brown eyes. This bear had one brown eye; the other was blue.

Naturally when the animals first met her they all noticed this and had their own little gossip about it. The cat, who had Chinese slits when he slept and Slav slant eyes when he was awake, frequently said in the beginning that he wondered just who her father had been whereupon everyone looked very grave. But the deer quickly came to the rescue, saying his grandmother had been wall-eyed, it was the word for it, and happened to some, but was no judgment and somebody else seemed to remember—now was it the mole?—that he had heard tell there was once an opossum with differing-colored eyes also. Since everybody knew the bear's eyesight was perfect and that therefore the *blueness* didn't mean *blindness* and since nobody could make a real scandal out of it, they soon ceased to talk about it, this fact of her ocular oddness, and if some never forgot it, like the cat, came to like blueness almost more than brownness. As a matter of fact, the blue eye grew on them all, becoming a dear basilisk power all on its own, so that when they looked at her they usually sought for the blue eye first, and who knows but that the Mary mantle hue of it and the heavenly shade wasn't the reason, along with a thousand others, why the bear held the power she did over them.

For she did hold it, yes she did. It wasn't just the fine meals consistently good as they were, and served up so nicely, nor the variety of the guests—after all, they had a bowing dove as well as a great grey goose, and a bird, too, with a wooden leg (the bear had snatched him from a weasel's jaws and with her own two paws put his left leg in splints) and a cat, moreover, who had taken the pledge and vowed never never to look at a bird (though the lame-legged one was a sore temptation) and a sheep rather famous for her glacial reserve, not to mention all the rest—it wasn't, no, in the clientele, nor the locale. Given all that, and granted it, how many beasts would have stayed on and on, forgoing a slightly more passionate life, had it not been for the bear? But the bear was there and she did run it, was there in their thoughts like fleas in fur and in their feelings like bees in roses. She was there and it was she, first and last. So that was it and that was how it went, and that was the evening procedure: music, or story telling or a constitutional to see the moon being buried or a poking about to hear the dew fall. But there would be other evenings too, what the bear called intellectual evenings, when the animals were apt to get very tired right away, though it did depend. Debates took less out of them.

Some such subject would be broached as: why are fur-bearing animals apt to be the chilliest? Naturally neither the bear nor the mole nor the cat took part but let him with what the bear called a leather skin, that is the deer, hold forth. Truth to say, his general ignorance both amused and pleased the three

14

who carried fur on them, since it is always pleasant to have one's own kind talked about. All three knew of course that they weren't any colder-blooded than the deer: it was merely that warmth made their fur feel better! whereupon the sheep stunned even the bear by baaing: Yes, but why don't *I* want a fire the way you three do?

There would be intellectual discussions, too, on hibernation and why the bear didn't have to. Progress! she said proudly. We have adjusted to the modern spirit that doesn't believe in staying in bed for six months. Everybody was very impressed. The cat might then want to know if the bears still chased sleighs in Russia. Wrong on two counts! she would say like a school-master, informing him of the correct procedure. But Russia is famous for bears, isn't it? the cat would persist with a sly wink. All places are, the bear might or might not say gloomily.

The cat would gloat as he had gloated before, since this was not the first time (it was nearly the forty-second time) he had found occasion to bring in the sound RRRusssha, whose pro-nunciation he had by now mastered perfectly. Not that the cat knew what RRRusssha meant (and heaven forbid him from finding out) or what it was, though he supposed it to be, as he supposed most things to be, just next door. But that he had had the sense to connect it with bears charmed, he did know, the bear. After all, he was the only one to show her that much curiosity!

For the bear talked over the heads of the animals nearly every one of those intellectual evenings and the animals didn't even notice it or wouldn't have cared if they had noticed it. What-ever she said sounded good to them and besides, they had their own notions to mull over. The bear's voice and expression set them off as music may the unmusical who, paying no more attention than, say, the sheep did to what the bear might be saying, have the pleasing sensation of being refreshed while reviewing some childhood memory, by the waterfall of a fine cadenza heard somewhere remotely in the distance.

So the cat was the only one of the lot who actually took in some of her phrases and actually thought about some of her words (such as progress! for example.) And whether or not he truly cared, he wanted to *seem* advanced, as a slit-tongued starling may *seem* to want to master a knotty sentence. The cat had a further little dim intuition, picked up who knows how, that there was something other tribes of animals mewed or baaed which was the great secret to thousands of things. And he had the words for it, he was positive. *Eng-ish! Eng-ish!* Wasn't it that?

Thus on the intellectual evenings he would get excited and silently meow or manipulating his tail like a fan lash himself into a perfect little flurry. Much in the way of ambition would then tumble over him—if, addressing the bear privately, he should personally challenge her about this thing! This unspeakable thing! Everything told him, from fox fire to cat's cradles, that she had to know! But alas, such seconds of mental activity would pass, leaving him somewhat more languid than usual, and, besides, the bear had spoiled him early. If their relationship had begun on another plane! Or if she had the steeliness of the sheep! he might, oh he might have exerted himself. As it was, her lap was the great hideout into which, when he saw her alone, he had to leap, purring at basso profundo as she called him Singer! Sweet Singer! Sing for your supper! Ah, he did, but he *might* have talked!

So that was how the evenings went. But soon enough, whether it was debates or stories or cosy interludes with everyone rubbing elbows, cheek by jowl, the bear would say time for bed! and off the animals would go, some to a turf cushion and others to fresh hay bolsters. . . .

Now one day when the bear was preparing for a fish party, the deer trotted in, antlers awry, and drawing the sheep aside whispered that he had just seen a hoofprint—a horse's hoofprint!—over on the next hill from the hotel. The sheep coughed and both put their heads together for everybody knew what the bear felt about horses. *No horses!* It had been her one edict, and from the beginning. Dogs she felt strongly about too, for hadn't they baited her forebears? But nothing could match that command: *No horses!*

Curiously enough, the cat began to dream badly, and exclusively too, of horses. One night he swore it was more than a dream and that he had actually heard a great trampling nearby. Don't trouble the bear, they whispered, as if the cat's fears weren't greater than the bear's.

The cat was right. Hoofprints were seen nearby, in the bear's bed of fresh French mint, as a matter of fact. The bear has enough to do and worry about, they said, out of the goodness of their hearts. So the hoof mark was carefully obliterated and the crushed mint pulled up, to the delight of everybody, for the bear dosed them with it on the least pretext. But still, was this enough? If the bear hadn't been sleeping on her good ear, she would have heard! So a little privy council was held during which plans were discussed as to how to ward off the horse should he be seen again and how to discourage him forever. The old deer bravely proposed stabbing him with one of his antlers, the sheep said she could butt and the cat not to be outdone said he could leap on the back of the horse and scratch, while the grey goose led off in a little oration about how horses had knuckled under and sold their birthright for a mess of hay, and so on, much disapproving talk, when nobody would admit the real truth, that horses were just *too big*. Since nobody took the old deer's suggestion seriously, nor the cat's either, it had to be left to the birds. Let them, always friends of the horse, go out in a delegation to inform the horse of the true situation.

Warn him of me! the feeble deer pleaded, and that goes for me, coughed the sheep. The goose said: If it were strength that counted, horses would be masters of the world, a truism rather too true for comfort, though the goose went on about platoons and maneuvers she would lead the birds in. In short, all hoped that the strong but stupid horse might be outwitted.

That same day the birds went drilling and were prepared the next day for a grand review, but that strong horse, was he so stupid? For though the birds flew all over two woods, they didn't find him. And the raids went on. A hoofprint here, a hoofprint there, that horse was circling nearer and nearer. In the meantime no animal told the bear although all of them marveled that she, so cagey about everything and with such an eye for detail, who was so capable about the vermin apt to attack a bird, and moths that might get into moleskin, or the deer's antlers when he was growing them and it hurt to cut new horns, that she so smart and noticing hadn't seen what they had seen . . . Unless it was a phobia? *No horses!* The way she had said it!

In any case, the secret was kept for several days. The bear may have wondered why the animals looked so sheepish when she came upon them unexpectedly but if she did, she had other things to think about. A new application had just come in from a three-legged fox (who had lost one leg in a trap) and surely anybody who had the courage to gnaw his way out of that deserved, she sighed, with tears of indecision about to swim in her eyes, a home like this? But she dreaded the thought of change. She loved the hotel just as it was. Everybody got on so well together and besides, what would the goose do if the fox came? She hated backbiting. What she wanted was peace, and didn't she have it?

She *had* had it, but nothing goes on forever, though the bear,

18

so wise, and clean as a cat—no bread crumbs in her brown beard!—was perhaps trying to forget this.

Now about twice a week or so the bear would set out to roam her property, taking a good look at all the berry bushes along the way and inquiring to see if her brook was in order. Usually she would stop to catch herself a fish or so, or puddle about with the stones, for she was a damned fine engineer, just as good as any beaver, or inquire to see if the otter had really set up housekeeping.

English walking-stick in hand, or alpenstock, the bear would climb up to the barley field kept especially for the old deer, and in spring when its green heavy heads would be waving in the good breeze, would as like as not make small leaps in the midst of it with a sober ecstasy. For she loved nature and would have loved a good piece of poetry had anybody bothered to read it to her. And from the barley field she would go up dogwood heaven into the bee glade where the linden trees stood, and listen to the bee music. Oh what was sweeter than that, with its bumblebee buzz and drone. And the bear would smile in her fur and lift her short muzzle up like a vintner drunk on his grapes.

It was on one particular morning when she had ambled from the bee glade into the birch grove that she saw the horse. But who would have known she saw him or anything had the chipmunk not been slipping obsequiously after her? That's how worried the animals were about the bear.

Well, the bear on beholding the forbidden one was at her most continental, for she roared forth a stentorian *Sir!* that caused the grazing horse to lift his head sharply. The bear stood her ground, leaning on her stick, a green bee veil drooping from that hat that she always wore when she carried her walking-stick.

The chipmunk was so excited he nearly fell out of the tree

and had to bite his lips to keep from chittering at what followed, for the bear in a series of majestic rumblings gave that horse a piece of her "mine." Or so she told them all later. The phrase puzzled the animals a good deal. Did she mean, they wondered, that she had a coal mine, or a gold mine, and if so, why would she give the horse a piece of that? It was not until the cat informed them that this was a higher form of rhetoric known as irony that the animals understood, though some, like the mole, still thought it meant she was going to give him a piece of her irony mine.

In any case, the horse was told to keep off in no uncertain terms, said the chipmunk, and that night at dinner the bear herself reported the incident, but with what a peculiar gaiety! Her blue eye positively glinted as she described the way the horse tossed his head and seemed to make a little bow before he cantered off. But he's a horse! said the cat, who had been biting his fur furiously throughout the whole rather indulgent recital. Yes, chipped in the grey goose, you said—

But the bear retorted quite rapidly for one who usually spoke with such thorough weightiness: He's not a horse, he's a colt!

This threw several and there was almost panic until the bear, allowing the deer to put his chin on her shoulder and the sheep her forelegs in her lap, informed them that a colt was not a different breed like, say, the donkey, but was merely a *young* horse. But young! she repeated. Younger than any of you! This left several of the animals cold; others like the old deer thought her remark in very bad taste, for who was older than any of them if it wasn't the bear? To add insult to injury, she concluded by adding, and they thought quite irrelevantly, that he had just lost his mother.

The animals were slow thinkers. It was not until the next day that it occurred to the sheep to wonder how the bear had happened to find out that that young horse had just lost his mother.

When she told the deer his antlers shook like a tree in the wind. How right you are! he said, always gallant to the sheep, and proceeded in his archaic way: It bodes no good, methinks. Why so? blatted the sheep, adding, in mockery of the bear, *Sir!* The deer who always looked flustered when anybody, even an old ewe, seemed to challenge him, hemmed and hawed and stammered: Why, you don't give an enemy a chance to make him feel sorry for you, do you? The sheep said *she* certainly didn't. Then neither should the bear! said the deer. The sheep felt this was an emphatic truth and the two of them wagged their heads. There's nothing we can do *yet*, said the deer as if inspired, but keep the cockles out of your wool! And he nudged her with one of his lower antlers. It was the deer's only joke. How many times had the sheep heard it, and every time she had to laugh out of the other side of her mouth. But this time especially. If the bear was going to go back on her principles, what was the use, dear lord, of believing in anything.

Not that the bear seemed to be, but there it was, the horse didn't go away, not at all, he came, or hovered, he lay wait in ambush, he stalked them all. A wonder he doesn't put his head in the bear's bedroom window! cackled the goose. I'd like to see that piece of her mine she gave him, chippered the cat. All of the beasts wanted to approach the bear on the matter but, wise one, if she let them into her lap, she also kept them in their places.

She was busy for one thing with her correspondence. It had staggered since the advent of the horse, for his hooves quickly broke many small trails that any beast would have the sense to follow. The increase of animal traffic past the hotel became stupendous! And besides that, the horse was most gregarious, and would talk to anybody, even a shrew, so that word got around more than ever of the hotel and its amazing facilities.

Therefore requests for information and applications from old veterans increased daily. Anybody with a conscience, and the bear had one, would have been troubled.

Soon everybody was miserable except the bear. That was the truth of it. Everybody had felt as she used to feel: what they had come for was peace and in her hotel they had found it. But now where was peace? Gone with that horse. The animals didn't know about all the bear's correspondence but how could they miss the traffic out there? Skunks, porcupines, all kinds of objectionable nobodies bowling past and with a really low and ignoble curiosity stopping to look in. A goat even butted at the door as though he thought he had the right to knock and a ram set up so much commotion that the ewe had to be delegated to lead him off. But she set her feet together and wouldn't budge. And the deer almost quarreled with her over her mulish obstinacy. Petty bickerings set up between the birds and the dove began to bow madly at the goose who took it as an offense. Nothing was as it had been. Peace! It was a phantom of last year, or last century.

And all the while the bear's blue eagle eye seemed shut. She apparently smelled not one rat. Or the horse for that matter, who came and went in a maze of errands with such an increasing insouciance that it was maddening to behold. Why, he seemed to toss his head all day, and pranced and pawed the earth with one fine little foot while the bear, rolling her eyes at this, looked positively asinine.

It had all happened so quickly, that was the trouble. First they had been so worried about the bear and had spent so much time trying to cover up and conceal the dreadful news which turned out not to be dreadful at all for the bear, only for themselves, and some even wondered if she hadn't known maybe all the time. It seemed at least that she ought to have asked their permission about somebody as big as that. The animals felt really burned up, and puzzled as well. It didn't seem like the bear to want a horse near. *No horses!* The command rang now in their ears almost mockingly.

The bear had always been a plain dealer and a straight shooter, and no one had ever caught her in an apology. If she did wrong she was quick to admit it—but then when did the bear ever do wrong? The animals couldn't have even imagined it until that horse came along. Before, when she would roll in as though she had just dipped her jaws in wild honey, what a jolly contentment emanated from her! What makes the bear so happy, the animals would ask, though they knew she groaned in her sleep. They loved to see her blue eye sparkle at little pinheads of shoots coming up. If ever the deer cropped her wild strawberries by mistake, thinking they were just flowers, how it grieved all the animals to see the kind way she swallowed her disappointment. Brave, forthright, resolute, independent, a fine manager with an endless knowledge of herbs, salad leaves, mushrooms and nuts, besides all the berries you could shake a stick at, an expert on fish and bees, of course, she was for them all their queen and their Rock of Gibraltar. And now to see a change begin, or some deadly little alteration . . . why it was enough to make them want to kill that young horse who had brought her to this. His thoughtlessness, his irresponsibility, the way he slobbered at meals when on those awful occasions he joined them for dinner . . . He ought to eat at least in a feedbag! said the mole who frequently showed a startling knowledge of the world. The other animals had long since been trained to be neat at the table. It bitterly interested them that the horse wasn't seeming to have to learn. . . .

Soon beast was snapping at beast in a quite shameless fashion. The stories at night got fewer and duller and almost stopped, since storytelling depends on the sense of an audience like any other art. The bear, however, was at fault there for after supper giving no excuse (but then when did the bear ever give an excuse?) she would take herself off. She was trying to keep up with her correspondence, but did the animals know that? Some put the darkest interpretations on it, while others, apt to be self-distrusting, like the old deer, thought she was punishing them for their attitude toward the horse.

Things went on in this way. The horse didn't come there to live but he might as well have. In fact, it would have been easier for the beasts if he had, for then they would have been more or less on an equal footing, with the horse to his own bedroom, and all that. This way, with his great license to come and go as he pleased, the horse was everywhere and nowhere. They felt his presence without being able to combat it or meet it head on, or even criticise it openly. Everybody admitted, of course, that the bear liked him excessively and nobody could understand why. While the old edict, *No horses!* seemed to echo like a hollow voice out of a woodchuck's tunnel.

It was a bad state of affairs, though not to the unseeing eye as yet, not to the bear's, the animals thought, aggrieved, let alone to that silly horse's. So bad, in fact, that the cat, who seemed to have lost his temper for all time, declared one day that he was not going to pay his rent any more. (He paid it in dead mice.) This shocked the deer, who had the courage to protest, moreover, but still the remark sank deeply into the memory of all, and more than the deer, chewing an old grass blade, or the sheep, working her cud from one side of the mouth to the other, looked as if they might be secretly contemplating rebellion.

Yet if one night the bear, deciding to give up on her correspondence, would return to the old way of the evenings, with sheep's face on her knees and goose in lap and deer patiently waiting to rest his chin on her shoulder, how ready the animals were to forget it all, even their lofty indignation about the horse, how eager they were to restore their Rock to its Throne.

Except for the cat, who ridden by fleas that he swore had jumped onto him from the riffraff going by all day, remained determined for revenge. No horses! No mice! he mock-mewed. He was true to his word though it meant also that he sometimes had to forego breakfast. Mice were not caught but flourished, first in the deer's room, where he liked to keep a bale of hay handy in case he got hungry in the night. In no time at all it became terrible for the deer. Mice would get into his ears at night and walk up his broad forehead to his antlers just as though the doddering old fellow were an iron deer, not a live one. The deer, not being the complaining kind, being very proud, in fact, of his sweetness, kept mum till the cat maliciously asked what were those scamperings he heard in the night? Could it be a grasshopper's minuet or a stag-beetle's cotillion, he cracked, which excited the goose to raptures. But the bear, overlooking a barrel of innuendoes, went on washing salad leaves for the raccoon as if she were deaf in both ears until, a few days later, it was evident, and must have been, even to her!, that the cat owed her mice—hundreds!—for everywhere you looked there they were, either sitting on hind feet, boxing with one another or nibbling at one of the chipmunk's nuts which in a fit of laziness he had cracked open and then abandoned, or chewing in a frenzy of whiskers at one of the old deer's ears of sweet corn that he kept in reserve for dreary months.

A showdown was due. Everybody except savages like the raccoon knew it, or odd undergroundlings like the mole.

And just as it became clear to all that either the mice would turn them all out or a hotheads' smouldering would leap into real factious flames of rebellion, the bear disappeared.

Oh how the animals felt that first morning when she didn't heave in for breakfast! They put two and two together of course when the horse wasn't seen either, though the birds to prove it went scouting over three acres at least.

A desperate, a desolate state of affairs! Rebellion was quenched instantly. Not even the cat thought of taking over or with a rival faction setting up his own hotel. Nobody cared for anything but that the bear be found. Small parties, expeditions were formed, bushes beaten, trees climbed, outsiders like the crow called in to scour fields and woods. All the trails the horse had beat down were meticulously followed. The beasts were really very thorough and almost scientific but their sleuthing was not rewarded.

Darkest of all days they had ever lived those animals lived then. Nobody ate anything to speak of, and how restlessly everybody slept at night with the cat up at all hours and the sheep coughing incessantly. The deer broke one of his antlers in a fit of grief and the mole took to burrowing as if he would revive the old and now scorned precedent of hibernation, but for grief's sake this time. The hay on the roof began to blow away since nobody but the bear knew how to plait it, and weeds grew in the beebalm. The bees themselves had more honey than they knew what to do with and petulantly asked for her every day.

And then one afternoon the raccoon who was always so touchy and shy that they hardly thought of him as a member of the hotel, and who had gone off as a matter of fact soon after the bear had, came slouching in and told them he had a story if they wanted to hear it. The bird with the wooden leg was sent to convene all the tenants together, and round they gathered by the dead fireplace where the bear had formerly regaled them. It was enough to bring short sighs of sentiment from even a stolid old ewe.

The raccoon was no great storyteller and had never in times past bothered to turn up at those assemblies, so that he had no experience, let alone talent, for knowing where to begin with an event and how to string it out in all its detail and the animals had to ask him and ask him, and fight to get things straight, with the beginning where it should begin, that is, before the ending, for truly this beast was the least trained of all their thinkers, but after some hours of agonized cross-questioning and repetitious tell-me-agains, the knots and snarls of the tale got unraveled and it went this way.

The raccoon had been poking along on the west branch of the brook over on the third hill—and none of their business, either, why he was rattling along over there. Truth to say, the chief reason why the raccoon told his story so badly lay in the fact that he was extraordinarily reticent about revealing *his* habits and private preoccupations. The animals thought it very egotistic of the raccoon to think they cared about his affairs when something so much more important was at stake! But the gist of it was that wandering there by that little arm of the brook he happened to enter a patch of turf that the trees hadn't yet taken over, though it was ringed round with small innocent birches, and there had seen the bear, seated on an old log, and the horse there too, but not cropping the turf whatsoever, walking, rather, on his *hind legs*.

But the most stupid thing about the raccoon was that nothing seemed to astonish him. He said that the bear sat on the log and the horse stood on his hind legs as if he were talking of salad leaves or another raccoon. It was this sort of thing that nettled the animals so much. What do you mean, the cat asked fever-ishly, walking on his hind legs? While the deer, thinking of all his additional burden of antlers, shuddered at the very thought of it. Is it possible? continued the cat, thinking too of the strain on the spine. Why there's nothing to it, said the grey goose, *I* do it all the time. You only have *two* legs, observed the sheep, always snobbish about her four, and the goose, up in arms, flapped one large wing to show what grand choice she *did* have. The raccoon yawned as the animals fussed on, and actually nobody asked him to continue his story for some ten minutes.

When he did, he had this much to say, that after the horse had stood up on his hind legs he would then go into a little motion with his four legs that the bear seemed to be tapping one foot to and nodding at with her head also. Again the animals took up this point separately as to what was meant by a little motion and why the bear seemed to be conducting it. The cat finally asking the raccoon to illustrate got only a snarl for an answer but the sheep, suddenly becoming very good and lively, got up herself, baaing eagerly: Was it like this? and with stiff joints tried to execute what might be called a schottische. But the raccoon wouldn't even look at her and when nudged to do so by the tittering chipmunk, barked out that they were all fools and he had no more time to waste with them. The grey goose proved she had a real gift for mediation by literally begging the raccoon to stay on for a moment though she had as much right to sulk at the sheep as the sheep had at the raccoon, and did produce a wise question: Did the bear look happy?

The raccoon at the door now replied that she looked the same as she always did, and some of the animals threw up their hands. That was just the point! The bear never looked the same! Everybody knew how changeable she was and excitable. When she laughed nobody laughed better or longer and it made you laugh just to hear her laugh, but hadn't they learned by now that a sigh often followed a laugh as sure as bees in clover? Oh they thought of her up on strawberry hill with her paws all stained by the wild red juice, eating quarts of the little sweet things, or in the crooked orchard, standing there in late summer, lifting up her short powerful arms to the apples red on one side and yellow on the other, and that was the bear when they saw her happiest, that blue eye set in her head like a madstone, but just as when she groaned in her sleep, it would begin to rain in her memory and then she would prowl around with

28

oh such a look! But there was no use in talking to the raccoon about that.

Everybody was dying to know if the bear had seen the raccoon or how long he had stayed or when he had left and why he did but what was the use, the raccoon would not be persuaded. That was his story, he said, and there was no sense going on about it, and left.

The raccoon's surly distrust of everything but merest fact made some of the animals feel very cheated, and a coterie withdrew for the purposes of further speculation.

If only we knew *Eng-ish*! began the cat, stalking back and forth in the room where once they had talked about the horse, and stopping then to sit down and pull at his front paw with his teeth, something the cat always did when he was thinking hard.

Eng-ish, Eng-ish, does the horse know it? twittered one of the birds.

The cat who had been at sword's point with them since the departure of the bear, who was in fact all but ready to forget the solemn pledge he had made never to disturb them in any way, so forgot himself that he lunged at the nearest one and the grey goose had to hiss at him for his wickedness so that once again the main point was all but lost.

But if the birds were too frivolous to understand the subtlety of the cat's remark, the old ewe wasn't. For though usually the last to notice language, something in this mispronounced thing flew like a magnet toward an old iron filing as she bawled the sound back, making a real hash of it, challenging: What's that, and what of it?

Alas, the ewe would never get a sheepskin for diplomacy. And first by her hard-boiled look she stared the cat out of countenance and next by her attitude of severe distrust toward everything and in particular the cat, drove every flicker and glim-

mer of the secret idea of the secret language the cat knew the
bear knew straight out of his head. Yet he did not completely
give up for bracing himself against the tree trunk he kept to
sharpen his claws upon, he reared up on his back legs, hissing:
What does she want him to do *this* for?

Well, the sheep didn't know, but she knew something else.
Everything in the cat's eyes and hedgework of whiskers told
her too suddenly what it was, and she sent sage glances to the
deer that warily he returned.

What did the cat know? But they knew, they knew! Let the
raccoon and the mole be ignoramuses, and the chipmunk too,
along with those birds who'd stay just as they had been born,
hopeless innocents! Let them think there was nothing beyond
it all, nothing outside their three hills and four woods but more
of the same! with endless animals living just like themselves
whether in hotels or not but eating and sleeping and being cold
in the winter and warm in the summer. Just let them think so!
But as for that, had the ewe lost some of her lambs so mysteri-
ously for nothing? And that young doe the deer had once
blubbered about in his sleep, what had happened to her in the
prime of her youth? They didn't know what it was, and really,
they didn't care to know, but they knew just the same that
there was more to it than all this, and wasn't it the wonder of
the bear that she knew too? The wonder and the darkness of
the bear!

But the birds, like provincial schoolgirls, must go into gales
of tittering again and swooping down past the cat call out:
Eng-ish, Eng-ish, does the horse know *Eng-ish?* whereupon the
privy council had to be disbanded in terrible haste with the cat's
first thinking on the real secret lost in fracas of grey goose,
himself, and birds.

And because it was lost, routed in fact, and the daring sound
flouted by birdbrains, and because everybody had had so little

experience, nobody could come to a sensible conclusion. They couldn't understand, they simply hated it, and especially their honest bear's double-dealing, her going behind their backs to meet that horse and then sitting there on a log and encouraging him to stand up on two legs when it was every beast's obligation to use the four given him!

It was this fact that they couldn't get over. They might understand her meeting the horse, they might if hard put to it, since after all she had asked him to dinner once or twice but what they could not understand was that she who liked to look beasts square in the eye when she didn't beam benevolently down on them should permit, no, encourage that horse to rear back his perfectly frightful weight and tower there over her. Bad enough that there was the inequality there was among the members of the species, so that a cat had to be dwarfed by a silly sheep or run around between the legs of a deer, bad enough, but that it should be augmented and heightened! Why, it seemed all against nature and it was only a proof of the raccoon's absolute lack of imagination that he couldn't see it and was simply grossly content to narrate the fact.

It was finally the deer who observed that the raccoon didn't *care* the way they did, even though the bear washed his leaves for him. And it was true, wasn't it? Nothing seemed to excite that raccoon. Read him any miracle and he would merely curl his upper lip.

So the animals were left in their little quandary with one half the hotel wishing the raccoon had not told his story and the other half soon believing he had made it up, for the mystery of it plagued them all and though it was late spring many of them shivered and all of them except the birds looked at the dark woods with slightly different eyes. *Eng-ish! Eng-ish!* Things they had not dreamed of! The hills beyond the hills and woods on woods!

Now new forays were organized with plans drawn up to make the trip to the sacred little grove where the raccoon said he had seen the bear. But first the birds were sent out to reconnoiter once more in the partially open field that connected their three hills and four forests with the rest of the hills and the other forests (or so these beasts *had* visualized their geography) and the lame-legged one came back with—oh but the animals nearly fainted when they saw it—a strand of their own bear's fur and chatter so excited that not even the other birds could make sense out of it. So, blazing a trail rather fearfully, the party of them made their way over rough terrain, hummocks and hassocks of grass, and a mean little quagmire and stinging bushes and Virginia creepers and honeysuckle tangle, to that open field.

All the way over, of course, the animals forbore from speculating on what that moustache of fur in the bird's beak could mean. They simply drudged ahead in single file, the deer clearing the way of spider webs with his antlers and the sheep following up in the rear. As grim a little procession, save for the birds whose high spirits couldn't be downed, as anything you might ever see. Moreover, many of them became very nervous since they had never been this far away. There were abandoned ants' castles that they passed, great sandy constructions empty now of all that industry, and fallen birds' nests and various frail shells of birds' eggs either chipped through or—who knows?—obliging the cat to look at them with sudden scavenger eyes. Worst of all were several little fine white skeletons. Nobody stopped to find out to whom they once might have belonged, but each one had his own thoughts.

Now there wasn't an animal that wasn't smart about directions when traveling alone. Put him down in the blackest forest and he would find his way over fallen trees and hollows where snakes curled up, oozing marshes and a twilight that went uphill and down, but this would be, too, because he wasn't doing it for a purpose, he was following his own sweet will and rambling by a sixth sense. The cat might take fifteen minutes to cross a small strip of an open field near the hotel when, if it had to be done, he could bound it like a jackrabbit in two. But what was the use of hurrying when every grass blade offered a variation all on its own with that insect life in the maze of it so animated and the whole of it such delight to each sense, especially if the wind blew? And life was so fascinating just because one did dawdle . . . So it was that each animal felt. But not this day. For one thing, they had an objective in mind, and that in itself made them jumpy. For another, too, they weren't used to going in a company and so became self-conscious or felt somehow perplexed and uneasy with it. It affected their instincts, too, that they had to keep more or less in a straight line and proceed methodically step by step when all were used to traveling the way a brook does, by the path of least resistance. True enough, it took them like the brook longer to get wherever they wanted to go, but again, what of it? Every brook may feel that its destiny magically and magnetically draws it to some distant river but does the attraction of that looming end oblige it to get there by that shortest distance, a straight line? No. The sense of other destiny is there all the way, in every flat or round stone the brook trips over, under every bush, tree or moss-ledged wall the brook passes by, and so it was with these beasts when they went out on their rambles. Every moment of the divaricating, very desultory direction they took was as significant to them, as bewitching and surprising as whatever it was they thought would be awaiting them. But now today with the realization that a patch of bear's fur hung on the twig of a bush beyond the last forest in the big field, they felt goaded on by a dreadful sense that nothing but it mattered and so they behaved in that half-world of the vegetable twilight. Vast orange mushrooms that ordinarily would have astounded the sheep, unused as she was to forests, club-foot ferns that the deer would have fallen upon in an ecstasy, great tree trunks straddling their way lodged with the plush of a finest moss, or rocks capped with it that the cat would have adored to lie upon, curiously twisted dead branch forms that might have been mistaken in the grey gloom for an enemy, the fall of a pine cone that could have made the chipmunk stand stark still or the deer raise one foot, all antlers on the alert, they scarcely bothered to notice. Instead, they filed along in a dogged though crooked little line, heads down, and eyes fixed on that floor of brown needles. Not a sound did they make—they could have been trotting in velvet shoes on velvet—except when the deer's antlers brushed against low-hanging branches, or the sheep sighed.

But just because they hoped to cross the forest at its shortest point and to follow a logical course and just because they had to travel together, they might have become as addled as humans and gone round and round in a circle had it not been for the lame-legged bird who, acting as aide-de-camp for the grey goose, came down at intervals to steer them straight. But this guidance too, for beasts so accustomed to self-reliance, only served to irritate them, and what with having to stick together in that big church of a forest where daylight was a perpetual grey-brown and all life but an occasional butterfly seemed to have departed it so that it was like a museum as well as a church, and what with having to be guided by a bird, they were nearly ready to jump out of their skins especially when, on passing a hollow tree simply packed with honeycombs, the deer lingered and stared. And thus they were ready to pant with fatigue when at last the tree wall thinned and let in light and more light and suddenly the full sky descended upon them and the field began! Here the sun was still shining with meadow larks flying before the grey goose. Joy and relief and sheer weariness overcame them all, and without a word the whole troupe flung themselves down in the warm wiry grasses and went to sleep. The birds looked almost the tiredest of all, and sat pressed together on the branch of a tree, some with heads tucked in and others holding their chins very high, as if sleep were a proud and very active exercise.

Heaven knows how long they slept but it was the sheep who woke first, and since the deer was faithfully next to her, he woke too and followed after her into the field, occupied by spiteful-looking poison ivy trees, with a few dogwoods on its fringes.

The sheep felt especially unnerved by the long trip and tired of all the animals, except, of course, the deer, and in a mood less to explore than to be away from it all set off very briskly with a manner that plainly warned: leave me alone. What was good about the deer was that he knew this without having to be told, and knew how to keep a patient distance as the sheep moseyed here and there in that absent-minded state best known as wool-gathering. But when she suddenly gave a short bleat, rolling her head in the air and then bleated again, he was at her side. The sheep's nose was quivering quite like a rabbit's as she lowered her head to the ground and then raised it, and the deer, recognizing that a crisis was on her, stared in a sympathetic silence. She bleated, she pawed, at last she flung herself heavily on the ground, then she arose and trotted back and forth and once she bared her old yellow teeth, a sure sign of emotion on her part.

The deer was right. Something had happened to the sheep. She was like one who inhaling some bitter fragrance seems to have crossed over into another life or by taste has stumbled into regions usually known only to sleep. The forgotten, the buried world had been set awake and the sheep gaped at its forbidden fury, and rolled her eyes like the bear, and sniffed, and turned her head in lurid fright from north to south to east to west, her brief tail shaking, and signed and snuffled and looked over her shoulder, and pressed her nose to the earth and looked up again. And so it went on. The lord knows what the deer thought but the sheep had been snared by a memory and tumbled head first into its bag that she might extract a single strand out of a welter of tag-ends and raveled pieces—old yarn from the days when she was a lamb and trailed her mother and the days after that when she gamboled on gawky legs and days later than that . . . and suddenly she had it. Those marks in the grass! Look at them! she commanded the deer. And he did, and half blind couldn't see what she meant him to. Full of sudden contempt she yapped: Do you see how the grass is pressed down? The deer then admitted that it was suspicious. It's more than suspicious! she bellowed like an old ram, it's proof! The deer could have wrung his paws had he had them, but the sheep only trotted off like a businessman, saying: Now we've got to find that hunk of her fur! And find it she did, simply by following the marks in the grass where it hung in a sad little tatter on— the birds were right—a bit of a thorn bush around which a spider had already begun to weave a gruesome web. Don't touch it! the sheep barked. Just consider how I found it! But anxiety had so dimmed the deer's eyesight that he confessed he couldn't tell heads from tails and would she please explain what she meant. The sheep snorted but asked him to sit down and when with trembling legs he had, she uttered in a low voice: Ang-ish! Ang-ish! The *sh* of it traveled down the deer's spine and in an echo as before, dream figures in some deep recess of who knows where began to seem to turn and move as if in another moment they might fully come forward. When I was young . . . she began. . . . After my lambs. . . . she began again. . . . my babies, you know . . . they were *kidnapped*. I looked for them like we're looking for the bear. I'll never forget. Don't

36

let me remember. Oh deer! And hacking with a dry sob, she fell against him. But soon master of herself she went on: There were marks like this in the grass, and I had seen what makes them. It's a contraption that takes animals away and it rolls over the ground like nothing on legs does. There's a whole other bunch, you know, of those who aren't like us. They don't have four legs, they only have two, like the goose. Don't go on! cried the deer. I will! said the sheep, for we can't tell the others. Why does that mark go so near this bush? They were up here, they kidnapped the bear the way they did my babies. I hope they did the horse too, the deer could only reply, in a desperate attempt to be funny.

For a whole world of evil had opened before him and his tender heart quailed and his soft sides shook. He could not doubt but that the sheep was right, for she who always had authority had double the amount when she talked of pressed-down grass and kidnapped lambs, and with what he remembered of his own doe, if he got no results but the addition of confusion, yet a knowledge seemed to be multiplied too.

All the way back and all the next day the sheep would not let him alone but prodded and galled him with queries and statements and horrible suppositions. The deer hadn't known what *kidnapped* meant though he did suppose first off that only the best people had it happen to them, like the sheep's two woolen blue-eyed darlings who were the prettiest and best lambs a ewe ever had, and like the bear who was, as they all knew, the *best* bear that had ever been. Which led him to ask hopefully what was the occasion for grief? Even if they didn't come back, a good thing had happened to them, hadn't it? For the best things had to happen to the best. What about your doe? snapped the sheep. But even so, she went on to inform him, even if only the *best* had it happen to them it didn't mean that it was *for the best*.

And she told him more, told him things she herself had almost forgotten until the sight of the wagon-wheel tracks (for even the words had come back to her) stirred up those dregs in the bagful of memory. Things especially about. . . . Oh how it tied in with the horse walking on his hind legs, for that's what *they* did and their skins were so strange, something like yours, she reproached the deer with, except that they put things over it and at this she remembered malevolently that because their skin was so bad they had to wear *him* and *her* and other creatures to cover it up and that there wasn't one of *their* own kind they didn't eat all the time! But at this the deer couldn't stand it and wouldn't have it and finally told her that if she didn't stop he would have to leave, for there was not merely the torture of thinking about what they might do to the bear with all that flesh and fur, there was more, there was at last the awaking to that spellbound and trance-like image when in a thunderclap of sound and in a burst of blue smoke his doe had fallen to her knees and rolled over and with her last breath warned him to run. Well he had, but who could endure to think on it? In short, such a world of mystery and suffering had flashed before him that all he could do was to stalk about, wearing a forestful of antlers.

As for the rest of the beasts, the disappointment had been brutal—all that great trek there and back for no other sign of the bear than a shred of herself. One or two had explored to the other side of the turfy field and had observed that the forest there was much thinner and who knows what happened to it or what spilled out from it but everybody recognized that they had come to the limits and bourne of their world and dared not go beyond —(it was an unwritten law). There could be only speculation which each one tried to suppress, especially the sheep, who recognized that the double marks in the grass led right up to the woods and rolled on through it, which inevitably meant that something happened, and something rather unpleasant, you could count on that, just over and through the young trees.

But each animal's own private philosophy came to the rescue or they might all have wound up their days just sleeping their grief away in the warm wiry grasses. Each animal was borne up by some private trust and secret strength so that each made the long way back in, as a matter of fact, double-quick time. For with each there was the hope, too, that she might have come during their absence, might be waiting for them, with chimney smoking and fresh fish and cropped barley and chickseed all on the table! A dream! A delusion fit only for spurring them on! They all felt it when they entered the hotel, vacant of all but those insolent mice.

And from then on things changed as each beast felt in his heart that the great days were over and their queen gone, and the resolution came to each one separately that there was no point in staying together if the bear didn't preside, and though the cat with a certain amount of sickly nerve dared to propose carrying on the hotel in the tradition she had established, no one even bothered to answer, for it was clear enough to everybody that each would be leaving by the end of the month. And just as nobody had ever said where he had come from, so nobody said where he would be going but everybody knew that the birds would not see the sheep again nor the chipmunk the deer, and so forth, that each would go out on his own separate track, even the lame-legged bird, and establish his own destiny. Up till now the bear had made everybody's destiny her business and her destiny, but who but a great-hearted one like that could do such? Since the animals were all fatalists and fairly brave people, nobody really whimpered but many a one secretly approached that patch of her fur, carefully placed on the shelf above the fireplace as if the shelf were an altar and that fur the most sacred relic of all, and many a sigh was shed for the great goodness that had come, had reigned, and had gone.

AND THEN, after days and days, a very little packet of eternity, in which everyone relived his own past and thought of the great fish parties the bear had thrown, and the honey rolls and the sweet corn roasts and the berry picking and apple pulling and the soirees when lightning bugs made dances with the glow worms accompanied by the fiddling of crickets and the solos of young tenor frogs, and all that good merry life of food and fine stories with the bear always busy, transplanting blueberries and blackberries and bringing in an apronful of nuts for the chipmunk, and scolding the bees and fussing at the deer for the grass he tracked in or the goose if she had wet feet, and laughing and padding about, courting the beaver, admonishing the otter or chasing him off and cuddling them all and laughing with them and then going off on her own meditations up to dogwood heaven, *she showed up.*

She showed up one evening! And the animals were in such a welter of memory and a stew of mourning that they almost took her for a ghost, and a ghost she was of her former self, for she had lost thirty pounds at least with her fur so ratty you wanted to cry or give her a good bath at once, and her left ear torn, a sore paw. But their bear! with a thick leather collar around her neck and a chain dangling down and a wound gaping there—their bear! And so glad they were and so worried and so glad that they didn't know what to do but to brew her some of her own French mint tea and get her bed ready, for plainly she had come from afar and was at the breaking point. The old sheep proposed a good rubdown and that was done by goosebill and cat's kneading paw, and then they tumbled her into bed, and there she stayed for some days with the raccoon on his best behavior and everybody running errands. And oh how well everybody slept that first night—at last, at last! And how good and busy they were in the daytime with someone tiptoeing in all day to watch her slumber. During the reign of sorrow everybody had been too dispirited to pay any attention to the mice or the vines half-strangling the stairway or the weeds in the beebalm, but now with her back the cat set at the mice with a will and the sheep bit the weeds out with her own yellow teeth while the birds helped the chipmunk tie the vines straight. So soon the hotel was in order and finally the bear was ready to get up with her torn ear mending and her coat freshly polished with beeswax though a hot compress of beebalm still had to be applied to her paw.

Oh it was jolly, jolly, it was hallelujah, with nobody thinking of asking a question till the bear was ready to talk, and nobody thinking, either, of what could have happened, so glad each one was that she had returned and the old order had been re-established. They didn't see until then, not a one, how much they had suffered, and how broken their spirits had been, how desolate their pictures of the future, and how lost their paradise. But with paradise regained they saw and they felt the wiser for it, especially the deer and the ewe, who thought they had lived three lifetimes but had come out on the other side. And since the bear seemed just as happy, there was festival and fiesta and picnic lunches and vast musical evenings with a strutting delegation of black-foot crows and a bevy of thrushes, redbirds and larks as well as that mocker, the catbird, and that true mocker, the mockingbird, and the sheep nearly split her lungs to vie with her imaginary rival, the goat, and the cat wauled as if possessed of the basest of passions, with the chipmunk doing what he could and the deer trumpeting forth in a memory of youth.

And wild strawberries that had just come into their own were heaped up on great platters for her, and even the raccoon obliged by catching her dozens of fish, from eels to trout, while enough honey sat around to sweeten a thousand imaginations. So it was good times all the time till the sore paw was no longer sore and the ear was almost as good as new, and twenty-five at least of the lost thirty pounds had been put back on her. And then one evening, after a particularly riotous dinner, she gathered them round and with blue eye glinting, proceeded to begin.

Now, as it has been said before, it was an unwritten law in the hotel that no animal spoke of what he had come from, or what he had done in the life he had lived before he came there to take up residence. An unwritten law that applied to each and every one, and above all to the bear. Ask me no questions, I'll tell you no lies. That was a part of it and another part too was the supposition on the bear's part and her guests' too, that nothing before the hotel could have been half so good as the life in it, so why bore and pain people by talking of it? Of course the stories in the evening got around that in their own way for all of them were hinged on actual experiences the animals had suffered or had heard about or observed, but since these were first and last stories, with all sorts of alterations and disguises in them, changed names and places, and stories, too, of stories, nobody had to be oppressed by thinking that he was hearing a real confession or the literal truth. And the fact remains that nobody wanted to do so. For life in the hotel was such a reality, and such a pleasing and various one, such a constantly interesting and fascinating one, that everything previous to it faded out and truly only cropped up in sleep. Curiosity, of course, had always been sharpest about the bear but half of this curiosity was idle playfulness, just a way of whiling the time away by wondering about somebody so much in their minds anyhow, and certainly the animals had long since been content to accept her at face value, and be thankful for it.

But this evening as she sat there, bursting with energy and jollity and surrounded by the mystery of her fabulous return as a saint is by his halo, they had to admit that they were simply on pins and needles and that if they didn't find out, and tonight, what had happened and where she had been, they would just die. And especially too, the horse. What had become of him? Who had even wasted a thought on him during the reign of sorrow, or even during the days when the bear slept on upstairs in her bed and they were so busy putting things to right and getting them shipshape, or even during the days after she got up and every day was strawberry day and fish day and green field day? But all events have their curve and every emotion has its law and now tonight they were ripe at last for a rage of curiosity extending in every direction and fervent to eat up the least detail, even concerning that fool and trouble-maker who had almost brought them irreparable grief and all but broken up their kingdom.

Both the sheep and the goose were pettish enough to insist that the raccoon be present that he might learn how a good story was told and perhaps realize upon what graciousness, cleverness, insight and generosity the accounting of it depended, and though the raccoon was good enough to come, goodness seemed to have done him in, for he soon fell asleep and all the sheep's prodding with a hard horny hoof couldn't seem to awake him. So he didn't learn how a good story is told and never did know, so far as they knew, half of what had happened to the bear.

Though it was an early June night a wind had come up bringing some half sprinkle of rain and the bear who loved a good fire the way she loved a good crop of barley and berries was only too happy to suggest that they build one for the sake of her former sore paw. So cat brought in twigs and deer was loaded with heavier logs that the beaver had thoughtfully cut and soon a fine bed of rosy wood coals was glowing, and around this the beasts were ranged. Many looked at her short broad lap with an eager and thoughtful eye but no one, not even the chipmunk, would have dreamed of cuddling up on it that evening. No. Everything to its place and each in its own time. She had a grand story to tell, that they knew, and she needed a proper distance for it, with her audience up there alert before her. And besides, who had sat on her lap since she'd come back? The grandeur of her disappearance was as much upon her as the halo of its mystery, and not a one of them who wasn't awed in spite of himself and therefore filled with a sweet and tentative reserve.

So there she sat, paws on the chair arms and blue eye glinting, a smile all over her fur as she looked at them and began: Well, my dears, drawing out the word *dears* in that singsong drawl that made the cat's ears prick up like the deer's and reduced the goose to an idiot stare of simple gratification, while as for the chipmunk's fur, it trembled in a little storm of pleased nerves.

And so she was off. Or they expected her to be off on the boundless track of time and miles that divided them from former bliss and present bliss. And the sheep curled her feet beneath her so she looked to have no feet at all, and the cat lay in the shape of the sphinx, with one narrow foot delicately dangling, and the birds sat passionately pressed together with the grey goose on the thickest part of the bough, and the deer was all akimbo in rapture. And the bear began and went on in that honeyed voice that came to her when she was happiest and launched as she was on tale-telling. And the animals listened as they did at first just to the curl and curlycue of her voice, not bothering to take in too much of the sense, which the bear well knew, so that she always gave them a preface and a preamble before she got into the gist of the matter. And it was the same tonight until set at last for attentiveness, they realized that she wasn't dealing with the horse as yet, or why she had gone away and how she had come back, she was dealing, rather, with things far removed, oh so far removed, in a forest but not a pine forest like the one they had sweated through, but a great oak forest, with the stoutest trunks all festooned with ivy and set with bullet-round clumps of mistletoe, big as eagles' nests, some of them, a perfumed forest but not resinous like pine, with the turpentine of it trickling and oozing down the tree's side, no, a forest perfumed with greenleaf sweetness and red berries growing in moss and streets and lanes and avenues wherever you looked of vast tall trees spreading overhead their long leafy arches, so that the sky was roofed in and the sunlight came down green, and it was always cool and sweet-smelling and neat! No brush, no tangles of bushes and little scrub trees growing where they had no business to be, oh everything cleared out and orderly, with just those great masters of trees, those true kings sending up their stout bodies and their long-flung branches to heaven! and there she had wandered and gone playing with her mother.

Her mother! Get that! thought the sheep and looked at the deer to see if he had. But the cat had if the deer hadn't, for he twitched one of his more than waxed whiskers in that way that always made the sheep want to baa. Well, her mother! And what a mother! That was all too clear as time went on in this large stately forest. All too clear, yes. A great mother, the greatest one a bear ever had, oh so kind, so wise, with an answer for everything and a knowledge of far more than a cub could question.

A cub! And even the deer got that, and looked all but pained, for if everyone present had had a childhood which if it had to be remembered, could be remembered, that was all very well

45

and to be expected. They were just usual, just animals. But the bear! As well expect to give the fire a father or the moon a sister! People like her didn't grow, they happened, they were given to the world full-fledged, magnificently equipped with bulk, stature, claws and wisdom from the beginning!

That demurring occurred to them all, everyone had his own little pause so that there was a gap in the continuity unfortunate indeed for suddenly trouble was brewing . . . and the season had changed, it was no longer summer with deep perfumes of ferns, moss and leaves, nor autumn with the gold all raining, it was winter and snow lined every bough and the floor was pure ermine and there she was, she had lingered to stare up at this criss-cross snow work when lo, she heard a most terrible crash, a snapping and creaking of boughs and a grand plop and then her mother's great roar, such a roar, enough to precipitate all the snow off the boughs and start a whole avalanche from the skies! And running after her mother's tracks she had come upon the tragedy, for such it was, her mother had fallen into a bear pit!

A bear pit!

For once all questions were rampant, not a beast that wasn't agog to learn what a bear pit was, and when they were told none of them but couldn't help gasping at the wickedness of it, oh the wickedness! Just wait! said the bear almost triumphantly and the deer said he didn't know if he could and she might have to excuse him if it got worse. True enough, there were deer's tears already starting in his eyes' corners and the bear to soothe him said that was all in former days, and she paused and brought forth with a rounded flourish, *in another country.*

Country, country, echoed the cat, for they lived in country, what did she mean, *another?* The chipmunk chipped in, drawing up once again an outline of their own geography. You mean, he said, another country is beyond the turf field—not that any of the animals had told the bear yet that they had been there. But if the bear wondered how the chipmunk knew about that, this was not the evening for investigation with so much else at stake and especially the important word *country*. And like a good teacher she tried to describe how this was across water, water, water, days of it and nights of it and weeks of it, and salty water at that, with fishes as big as circus tents. But at that the animals stopped her again and the bear seeing how she had been caught up on the hook of her own worldly experience had to laugh and say just wait.

Then how big? persisted the cat, and the bear said as big as from the hotel to the first hill, whereupon they all gaped at her like ninnies and the sheep looked disapproving, for obviously the bear was kidding them. But she didn't say so, let the others be fooled, she was content to ask dryly had the bear eaten a fish as big as that? And how the bear laughed! until the grey goose, simply giving up on the ideas of *country* and *water*, croaked: But what of your mother in the bear pit? And the bear looked grave and said it was too bad to remember, for trappers in whiskers and boots finally came after she'd spent all night in a tree calling down to her mother who wasn't hurt but who was perfectly furious for she couldn't get out; yes, trappers in whiskers and boots had come the next day and surprised her as she was leaning over the pit trying to think up ways to pull her mother out of it, and heaped a net over her, and oh such a time as followed!

Carried off in a wagon? interrupted the sheep with a peculiarly tense voice.

The bear who seemed to have been lost in a dream nodded vaguely which the sheep took as a yes, and poked the deer.

But that was just the beginning of the bear's tale. Caught in a net, carried off in a wagon, transferred from stout man to stout man, most of them bearded, many of them booted, her grief had no ending but endless beginnings and she wasn't going to haul them over those coals. Bad enough for her to think of, including the fate of her own great mother! But eventually she landed with a dark swarthy fellow, a gypsy, she thought, who trained her to dance, and since she was young and loved motion and action, she didn't mind really at all. It was a good enough life with the crowds and the laughter awaiting her if she did well— and believe me, I did!—threw in the bear with pardonable enthusiasm. I saw to it that they chuckled and half the time roared, and I loved that, I did, being most foolish, and nothing could stop me from making a clown of myself and mocking the whatness of bear.

What's that? asked the cat.

Oh, murmured the bear, something I picked up in Germany, though actually I'm a Bohemian bear.

But at this point not a beast peeped and they were all, as a matter of fact, ready to give up asking. So many names for so many places and all this confusion about water, water, and country that wasn't country, and whiskers and wagons. They wanted their expanding world shrunk down, that was the truth of it, it simply tired them to hear so much: why, they couldn't even get all the first part straight where the mother fell into the pit, let alone that thing she called a fair one time and a circus the next. And as for men and gypsies, wasn't it all the same? Just a part of what they wanted to go in one ear and out the other, and some twitched and others shifted position very restlessly while the raccoon was frankly snoring.

The bear saw all this but she didn't care. She was launched on the sea foam of her own memory and sprung from a lissome bough half into the sky, the hot fervid lights of the circus were on her and the foul odors of that massed crowd, all tilted faces and bared shining teeth and those places where the eyes gave out light with that sound as from one throat of a beast more

48

angry than she until she learned better and knew it meant gold clinking into her master's cap and lumps of sugar instead of whips and proddings with sharp-pointed instruments. Why a bear in a hollow and down dogwood lane knew that—how not to ruffle your master's fur till you gave him the last big hug! But she had to work up to all that, and first it was shuffling in open streets, near markets of chickens and geese and fruits with a donkey braying as you went into your first two steps or a horse whinnying in a collar of bells and little ones standing around and big ones pushing and all their mouths open in surprise when her master squeezed the accordion and she, moved all beyond herself, tried to leap like a soul flying out of her great fur flesh. Then it was she had learned what served her a lesson for life: when she was most serious they thought it most funny. What were you going to do with that? How she had hated at first and wept tears of hot shame and learned only late that it didn't matter—each to his tears and all for their fears— life was just a big round in a circus ring but it all slipped back, it all turned again, it all came home if you hung on, and bided your time—any sheep down dogshead lane knew that!

So she went from country town to town, jingling and shuffling with a chain on her neck and a cap on her head and went home with the gypsy at night into a straw-filled cage simply hopping with fleas and pulled in a wagon by a horse more cadaver than horse, with sores and welts and bones all over, a horse that the master lashed when he wanted to and kicked when he didn't, and it was just nip and tuck, just nip and tuck! until she was lucky enough to be kidnapped. I've been kidnapped three times! she added.

But the second time was the best and she assisted, she did, by not growling nor baring her teeth but going as meek as any ewe's lamb with the man who unlocked her cage in the night. And this man was good, he taught her so much, all that she knew in one line. . . She tapped with a red and white drum, wearing a tall fur cap on her head, and she sat down at a piano and picked out a tune, she learned all kinds of new steps and dances so that soon she was in a troupe of other beasts too, terriers who made high dives into nets and jumped through hoops, of course, and lions who sat on stools and snarled at their keeper with his long black whip.

And not one of the beasts asked who were lions, nor went into it precisely about terriers nor queried her on the tigers that turned up nor the elephants of dangling trunks. The sheep thought she lied and the rest just thought: we'll ask sometime, languidly, as if sometime were miles away, while the deer thought, flank next flank of the sheep: I know who she is and the bear, and that's enough.

Well then, said the bear, they brought in a horse.

Oh what a quivering of nostrils beset her and them!

He had a black body with white spots on it and the finest small ears and the biggest dark eyes and what feet and legs. In all my born days I never saw anything so fine, and they called him Twinkletoes, a name I hated. A born chap for the business, all said. Perfect genius in fact, though not bred to it. It happens like that. A horse is born in some stable or so, on some farm full of mire and mud and chickens with his heart set from the first on something else and his calling confounding and perplexing his blood. Pity that horse who never gets out! Who follows a plough share spring after spring, in a muddy straight line, or with broken knees waits in the field while they toss up hay. Pity the one in a city who pulls a cab for fools with money to spend. Life that might have been splendid is not and all because he has missed the bus, he was born in the wrong stable after the door got shut, and all his fire and showmanship, his vanity and his beauty gone for naught!

She paused and the chipmunk yawned.

This fellow was lucky, she went on. Lucky and plucky and he took to me like fish run from otter and I to him like a lark to bees. So they had us in an act in no time, with me holding him by the reins and he weaving after me, tossing his head on that swan of a neck, and making the most elegant turns with his feet. Back feet never bothered front feet with him, he was Jack the Nimble and Jack the Quick and snorted and put his ears flat and pretended to bite—I was never taken in nor was he. Then I learned a small rhythm on the striped drum, and I beat it out to the horse's steps. It wowed everybody. They whistled, they roared, they threw up their hats and half of them lost them, it brought down the house, as the saying goes, and we became famous, and moved from city to city, working our way from Prague to Paris, and stopping in Austria, Lyons and Arles. What a life! Sometimes we stayed only a few days, sometimes one, and then off we were, packed in cages and wagons to be jolted and jogged all ways in the dark. And it got so we hated to be parted, that horse and I, so the trips became extra tiresome, it got so he took all his pleasure from me just as me with him, the hours we spent talking! How he improvised and extemporized!

He hadn't been kidnapped like me two times or torn from his mother on a cold morning, but sold, quite legitimately, and the horse remembered the dickering between his master the farmer and the ringmaster, and knew when to paw the ground and roll his big eyes till the whites showed, so you can say that horse had a hand in his own destiny and practically arranged for his own career. Well, but for talking to him all those times between acts and on the road, I might have forgotten what had happened to me for so much had with so much traveling and such a confusion of owner on owner, and whippings and lock-ups and crowds stamping and pushing and though I told you I took to it like a crow to a cornfield this really wasn't true in the beginning. I just danced because it hurt more if I didn't. But all the while my heart was with mother champing there in the bear pit, raving and grieving and shouting up words to me, wouldn't you know, every minute she was down there, telling me to climb a tree—make 'em cut it down to get you, she joked —and advising me how to make tracks for the hollow in a way that would put them off and advising and consoling and warning—oh never a thought of her own predicament—and at last as dawn came giving me her own philosophy in a nutshell for she thought she read her fate true in those slippery walls. Though I never believed it, never thought they could get her. And was such a rapscallion they had to clop me and foist me headfirst into the wagon and stun me. So when I woke up we were traveling fast, in darkness, and where was my mother? But I never did believe they got her and kept looking for her at every fair, thinking that was what bear pits were for, to get bears to dance like mother and me and it would be only a matter of time till she'd turn up, though actually I expected her to be a part of the crowd, not up there like me.

The bear chuckled. I guess I forgot what consternation that would have caused if mother had come ramping up, elbowing her way and swatting left and right, knocking so many heads together like peas in a pod and nuts in a basket and roaring like thunder, every tooth showing, just to stand in first row to watch me, her cub, who had come so far and done so much at an early age! I guess I forgot! But oh! what a sweet dream it was and—the bear beat her deep chest with one paw—it sustained me, *my dears*, my children, it held me up, because of this folly I could endure!

And now the beasts, so gratified once again by the sound of *my dears*, stretched quietly, and the chipmunk and cat drew nearer toward that short broad lap and the deer all but wondered what she would do if he dared once again to think of resting his chin on her shoulder. It remained as it had; the bear could have been talking of angels for all they really understood and had any beast been asked to draw up a map of the new geography he would probably have put it in air with water, water, water, standing topsy-turvy above them in sheets and standing ponds of it and Germany and Prague and Arles and Bohemian written on clouds that drifted by or dissolved in the wink of a lash and lion as much like griffin as horse is like unicorn. And because these place names and beast names soon bothered them no more than the bear's big words on the intellectual evenings, and penetrated no farther than a needle stabbing an alligator, they came to enjoy this stuff of reference, and felt as familiar with the words *circus* and *pirouette steps* and *piano* and *gypsies* and *gold* as those of us feel familiar with Betelgeuse and Altair and stars that take a million years to send their light down to us.

True enough, the goose felt very puffed up about one reference she had a visual equivalent for, and that was when the bear said that the horse arched his neck like a swan. Not that she was having any truck with that horse! But she did know, though heaven knows how, that the swan was a distant and somewhat inferior cousin of hers. Privately of course she felt miffed to think the bear hadn't said he arched his neck like a goose and arched hers so much up there on the bough that she almost fell off and did discommode the other birds. But after a moment goose forgave bear for this oversight, seeing that the creature was wrapped up in her story and just out of this world, just out of it!

Well, the bear went on, I told the horse some of my past—not too much for fear that he wouldn't *understand*—and she gave all the beasts a searching glance, but told him enough so *I* didn't forget, and could keep it straight in my own mind, and I suppose it was good for me. In fact, I'm sure it was the only way I held on to my sanity. For, for all the glamor of my life once it became successful, and there *was* glamor in spite of the falseness and cruelty and imprisonment of it, my roots were forever right there in the bear pit, with my own mother, and there in the forests where we had roamed and where she had taught me so much, where grey wolves slunk by, creatures far worse than dogs, with ghastly yellow eyes—oh not like yours, my sheep, they are pure gold of wasp—but spectral, evil, demon eyes and teeth—why, mine are nothing beside them! And she let the beasts see her stout long teeth again.

Once, she murmured, a wolf came up to me when I was playing with ground pine leaves—how pretty it was the way they laced and looped across the forest floor like ribbons purposely tied there! And I was such a fool that I held out some of the leaves to him, and even some berries I was saving for mother. But I will say, I will indeed, that pure innocence thwarted evil that time, for he slunk off like a long grey shadow. Or perhaps he smelled mother. For she soon came, and when I described him said I had maybe done right but only luck let me get away with it. It's not *really*, she told me, a just world, and you may consider your claws and teeth a blessing or curse but it's not all in the way you look at it for minikins dear, that's what she called me, they are a *necessity*. Now as to how you use them, that's something else. . . .

The bear paused again and swept the animals with her look. Something in the spines of the deer and the sheep and the goose quivered and curled and sent shoots of fire everywhere, though not a one betrayed it.

Well! the bear went on briskly, I decided right then and there to follow in my mother's footsteps and stick to *berries, honey,* and *fish*! How she did enunciate those three words and how the animals did draw breaths of relief as the terrible crisis of the unmentionable got passed over.

54

The bear drummed her claws on the arms of the chair. So that's how we're trained, by precept and loving example. I never, just for that reason, dreamed of attacking one of my men, beard or boots or all. Though I knew that I could, which saved me a lot. And perhaps I taught the horse that, and gave him a better character too. For I did say, you're stronger than they by far, you know, but why take advantage of it? Pity them instead with their bad breaths and backaches—show a firm hoof, but don't kick with it, dear, you could knock them too easily galley west. Naturally that fellow returned the compliment and we laughed, we did, at our own awareness and our own realization, too, of our strengths, and it amused us, too, that we were the means by which those men lived. We were keeping *them* though they, the fools, thought they were keeping us! For who brought in the gold, what made them famous if not our fame? We had our faces plastered everywhere—just think! all over Paris, with me in an apron and a tall fur shako and him with beautiful neck arched, doing a dance step. They gave us names which I'd like to forget but can't really—Hansel and Gretel—fancy me called Gretel!—and it was Hansel and Gretel everybody was bidding for, and Hansel and Gretel everybody packed the *Cirque d'Hiver* for, which is in Paris, the center of an animal's professional life.

Oof what odors! A mess of them! For they tried to camouflage the worst of the man smell by squirting some sickly cheap chemical perfume all over the place, a mixture of carnations and chloride—if I came back a thousand years from now I'd still be smelling it—but of course it couldn't drown lion piss and tiger sweat and monkey effluvia. And those monkeys! What disgusting cousins to my so-called keepers! And I must say, that sustained me too, and kept me sometimes from sinking my teeth in somebody's neck, just the thought of what *they* had come from, what low, filthy ancestry, compared with mine and that of the horse, compared with my mother, so large and noble, with people fighting to wear her fur, and the horse that men prided themselves on mastering and prided themselves if others could think they sat on him like they grew out of him and were one with him! And that fellow! When his skin would be in a lather of sweat it was as though he had on a silk skin, and I swore and swore that outside of my mother nobody had been born so beautiful. Why, his legs alone! People compared a woman's fine legs to his when they really wanted to put out praise!

. . . So we chatted and chattered and told our stories, and remembered and reminisced, and made up jokes and had such a friendship that mares couldn't stand it, let alone bears for that matter. Of course our act was one of the last and sometimes *the* last and we wouldn't have anything to do for some time after the show had begun and so I would sit in a cage off in an ante-room, and the horse would be tethered with a gang of others next to a giraffe sometimes, and my deer, you remind me of him.

The bear smiled so benignly at that that the deer knew it was a great compliment and flustered, lowered his head. Then the sheep had to know what the giraffe was like that the deer deserved this, and was told of his marvelously dappled skin, and the delicate knobs on his head, quite like a peacock's small top-knot plumes, and his wonderful liquid gentle dark eyes, and his purple tongue! Oh! such a tongue, so insinuating and supple and languorous! Oddly enough, the bear refrained from mentioning that most striking feature of the giraffe which is naturally his neck, and if this was out of defense of the giraffe, lest the animals laugh, or defense of the deer, lest they sneer at him for not having such a neck as that too, who will know?

Well, she went on, we would talk together, I mean the horse and I, even in that roomful of animals, some of whom behaved quite badly, especially the lion who would roar on purpose to drown out our remarks, and sometimes the giraffe would join us for the horse liked him too, though both of us pitied him. He was too wild and tremulous, too sensitive altogether for that life, and when they would whip him to drive him into his stall I couldn't stand it and would roar too, and shake my bars like any ape. And finally, do you know, the horse and I decided to let him loose, to free him! For we saw he would die otherwise. Listen: he had no act, there was really nothing they could do with him except to exhibit him for children to stare at. We thought even a zoo would be better, anything but this confinement in such stink and chatter, such a Noah's ark of all the animals from all corners of the earth when that wasn't meant to be! When, if you look at it, animals are separated by water and mountains, by heat and cold, by vegetation and compass, by continent and continent and country and country!

And she would have waxed more philosophical than that had not the animals interrupted her to say: Well, did you free him?

We did, she answered, and it was our downfall. Out of good grows evil. So my mother told me. So it was true.

And she sighed and paused and said: I *can't* go on. And suddenly stood up. Time for bed! And when they protested, cried: I'm so tired! Whereupon they all said: Of course, dear bear! And the deer heated a hot brick for her out of gratefulness for that flattering comparison she had made.

The bear slept deeply since she had talked so long and remembered so hard but for the rest of the animals it was sheer restlessness and tossing every which way all night. Countries marked them, chased them, howled at them. The deer slept in Paris and perhaps with the giraffe, the sheep in Bohemia, the chipmunk in Germany. Arles! cried the goose, while the rest of the birds flew from Prague to Paris and back again all the night over.

The cat couldn't even pretend he was going to sleep, and just stayed up the rest of the night walking back and forth in a fever of meditation. He knew he was just as beautiful, and everybody admitted that he was clever. If one practiced one also could walk on one's hind legs—suppose it did hurt the spine? Wasn't it worth it, that life of glory, and all that travel from Lyons to Prague and Austria and Arles, all that hand-clapping, those shouts of approval, that adoration of galleries, faces on faces in a bare row, teeth shining, hats flying, those other animals stampeding with approbation! The hairs on his tail swelled out at the thought of their calling for him—what would he call himself by the way?—and keepers doffing their hats before him and managers clamoring to sign *him* up, the extraordinary and only hind-leg-walking cat, the one and only who could do it in—boots! Boots she had said! Then let it be Boots!

And from hind legs he might leap—and why not?—fly through the air, to land—for hadn't she mentioned it?—on a trapeze, and from one trapeze to another trapeze till he reached the top of whatever that thing was they performed in, and the whole audience would lose its breath watching him, and ooh and aah when he swung there wild as a bat, and die again when he descended, from daring trapeze to trapeze!

And so excited the cat became that he nearly fell off the chipmunk's wall with the feel of that descent in his fur, and for the life of him, thinking about it, he couldn't tell whether it was animals he saw sitting there row on row, laughing and stamping and clapping, with the Bear in a special regal box, draped in red, or gypsies and men in whiskers and boots. He finally decided that because the bear had danced for the latter he must too, but he also had to admit that if he could really choose it would be beasts he'd prefer—but heavens, as though they paid!

58

The animals had had a day of it when they met with the bear the next evening. More than the cat had been disturbed, excited. And if they had not gone rapturous with dreams of the self and fame, it was for those simpler souls that some aura from all that talk of hot burning lights and noise and odors descended upon them and mixed with the good country air to entrance them and to alter it and to subject them in very certain ways to its spell. They didn't become dissatisfied with the hotel or their former lives—oh it was far from that—but they knew now as they had never known before that there simply was another life. And it wasn't the Prague or Paris of it that so enchanted them or those whiskered hallooing audiences, it was as much the bear pit and the wolf and the bear's mother and the giraffe that thrilled in their blood and blew some little kind of ghost music which died away and came again in gusts of greater sweetness, like a flute heard on the last hill or blown from elfin horns by some stealthiest brook in the depths of a wood, like what awakes a bird to sing at night when even he must know the dawn has miles to come.

If they had loved the bear before, they revered her now, from matriarch she had grown to sovereign *assoluta*, she prowled now in a dimension that gave upon dimension like vista on vista and where she went, their real, dear bear, went as if behind a veil, a mist, a glittering spray of illusion, their absolute, their ideal bear, who had lived so much and loved too, and endured such vicissitudes with such fortitude.

In a word, the animals were just overwhelmed; they had present and past to reconcile, vast crowds and their own poky solitude, the rural with the metropolitan, the foreign with the familiar, when formerly all life had seemed one, all origin here on their three hills and in their four woods.

Dinner had been especially splendid that evening but it was not cool enough for a fire. The bear gathered them around with alacrity, as though she had been living too for the *dénoûment*. And also, and also, for the more pertinent facts relating to her disappearance. Deer ranked by sheep as formerly, dove next to lame-legged bird, goose at the head; cat, chipmunk, mole in as usual, triad. Only the raccoon who had missed so much by falling asleep stayed away. The cat fastidiously crossed his very dapper paws, ears peaked like tents, and green eyes burning. Chipmunk and mole simpered together with picturesque sympathy. Everybody, needless to say, was on the *qui vive*.

The bear drank it in, she lifted her muzzle, smiled in her fur and began.

Did I forget to say, she started off like one who interrupted in a most complicated narrative by a long tiresome telephone call has the presence of mind to pick up at once, words and all, the thread of the last sentence left dangling: Did I forget to say, she repeated, that back of the *Cirque d'Hiver* was a grazing field for us beasts? Naturally nobody could keep us cooped up forever and since when an animal went to the *Cirque* he stayed on for weeks or months if he was any good at all, that field and its liberty was a necessity. It kept us in decent health for one thing, and believe me, any trainer loses money on a sick animal! And for another, it kept our tempers even and our spirits up. We got so we looked forward to it, poor prisoners, as much as we looked forward to our dinners and sugar-tits. But there's always a drawback and this one was that I couldn't be out there with the horse since he and a herd of others always went together. Of course it amused me that they classified me with the lions and tigers, seeing to it, I mean, that I was put out alone, but even so, a reputation if only for ferocity seems like a poor consolation when it's company, and specific company, that you want. But the point is that if the horses were bunched up together and left to trot around in assortment, the giraffe was also let out with them, and this is how my Rex, as I always called him in private, struck up the friendship he did with that fragile creature.

Now when things got unbearable for him, I mean the giraffe, because they the keepers whipped him so much, I said to Rex we've got to free him *but how*? Both of us knew the field was no good, bound round as it was by a stout high wall. Well, Rex thought at once of the answer: a corridor led, as he had observed, from the antechamber along and around and eventually out to the street. It was the giraffe's one chance as we saw it, to get out on that street and run, for he was fast as a horse when he had to be, and run for the Zoo. We figured, let him throw himself on the mercy of the world. Somebody seeing him with his dappled skin might even want him for themselves and in any case he would have gambled and even if he lost, anything was better than the life he led, and what's it all for if you don't take chances?

Well, at first the poor fellow was horrified when Rex told him of our plot, and said he couldn't dream of it even. We understood why. He was from so very far away, and had no more business being in Paris than I'd have being in the White House. But Rex kept after him and I got in my licks too when I could and eventually that fellow said—and, oh deer, I hope it wasn't just to *please* us—that he was ready to try it but how could it possibly be done?

We had thought of that! There was the moment in the morning when the horses were untethered and driven off to the field I spoke of, and the moment soon after when the giraffe's box was unlocked and he, harassed by keepers, was pushed and prodded in the same direction. Now: Rex was to stall and stall, and rear up, and whinny, and cause all kinds of commotion just at the entrance to the field when, by that time, somebody would be leading out the giraffe. Timing! You see it would depend on that. And while Rex was making a fuss, I would begin to bellow and roar—believe you me, I had the memory of my mother, and knew how it ought to cannonade—and strike out through the bars with my paws, and lunge at them, do everything that a good pacific bear never does, and altogether so startle and so confound them all that the giraffe with one kick and a nip could break loose and be on his way.

We were taking chances too, both of us, and the moment the giraffe saw that he was persuaded and with sweet thanks called us his benefactors and said he didn't know why we cared so much when none of the other beasts did but we waved that aside and said—for liberty!—and wished him the best of luck. Well, it went off, and much as I have described. Rex proved himself a very devil and almost seriously hurt somebody, the giraffe did manage to take a kick at the fellow who'd pestered him most, and I howled my whole heart away. The commotion was just as we had predicted—not a keeper but didn't lose his head—and greatest of all our luck, and the one point we had kept still upon, for it seemed almost the unsurpassable point— that door that led to the street from the corridor was *ajar*—to let in fresh air, I suppose—and the giraffe got out.

The bear laughed and laughed.

It made all the newspapers, she said, and *Figaro* carried a picture of him! Some humanitarians observed welts on his pretty hide which is far more than we had hoped for, and believe it or not, my children, he ended up his days just where we wanted him to—at the Zoo in the *Jardin des Plantes*!

There was much cooing and purring, quacking and chippering and coughing at this, for all the animals had associated the giraffe with the deer and had somehow been convinced in their hearts that only ill luck could attend him, and the sheep so forgot herself that she personally congratulated the deer.

So there was a cosy interlude and a gay one before the bear took up her story again. It was needed, oh truly so, for hard times followed fast on foot. The animals indeed had to pay for the good fortune of the giraffe, and as justice would have it, lion suffered as much as culprit bear and horse. For some days everybody was doubly confined, whips whistled in air, time in the field was brutally curtailed, and the keepers eyed every beast with surly suspicion. At first, the bear said, we didn't mind, being so cocky and thinking ourselves heroes, especially when it got bruited about that the owner had had to *give* that giraffe to the Zoo lest a rumpus be raised over his welts. Not that we *were* treated badly, she declared earnestly, for one thing they couldn't afford to. A mistreated beast just won't perform. But there are little nagging ways, you know, little snide ways of intimidating, like what they did to the giraffe which, if you have a highly strung nervous system is just as bad as a black-snake whipping. Well, suddenly Rex and I got aware of all this, of all the pullings and haulings and yankings, of the way the keepers called us brutes and made my collar tighter than it need be and flicked me with the loose end of the chain when I was walking, or curbed the bit too tight for Rex and reined him so close it pulled his head much too hard for comfort when, besides, it wasn't needed, his spirits were so high. All that. Somehow it began to get under our skins, after we'd freed the giraffe, this unceasing surveillance, this endless locking and bolting and chaining. It got so when we saw that corridor where the giraffe had made his great dash for liberty, my fur would begin to stand on end, and Rex would paw earth, his eye rolling, and it was just as if that wild time when we freed him lived its life on and on in us. We smelled the outside, we did, even though the door was closed, and every time that chain tugged my collar it was like telling me: ho! here we freed the giraffe! why didn't we free ourselves too? The thought ate at us, hardly without our knowing it, and it got to be the same way in the ring. We'd been in our act for some time by then, and knew it cold, knew it so we could dance in our sleep, and did, sometimes, and now with this notion of what we had done and what we could do if we wanted, it got so we cut up without knowing it, adding steps here and a rhythm there, like experts who know how to take every trick. And Rex kicking his heels higher and higher, like feeling his oats, you know, and both of us beginning to feel truly ourselves and not belonging to anyone, or beholden, either.

Not that we figured on running off, it was just the idea that the giraffe had and we could if we set our minds to it. It made us hilarious, no end, like the thought of dancing new ways, dancing in dozens of ways, different ones every day. As it was, how nervous the boss was getting. I'm sure he thought: animals are so unpredictable! When all we were kicking about was just the routine men seemed to expect!

Well, it went on in this way with ourselves more larksome though we *were* reliable, when what does the boss do but up and die.

He owned us, he owned a string of ponies and some camels and zebras that performed in a very dull desert act, and Bosco, the tiger, and Fanchette the lion. And the day of accounting came. A tall red-faced fellow who smoked a cigar and blew the smoke right in my face said he'd buy us and Bosco, but nix on the rest, and he was ready to settle for just us two. There was talk of Madison Square Garden, which made Rex and me sit up and take notice. A garden! Did he mean we'd have fresh berries and sweet corn? That made us feel really good and we thought some less about liberty.

Everything happened very fast then. Before we knew it we were packed up and off in a wagon and next on a thing that took us across water and water. That's what I was telling you. Days of it, nights of it.

And you ate a fish, the sheep began.

The bear held up her paw. I didn't! There was a storm. Nobody ate. Nobody could. A terrible storm that rolled us all every which way. I didn't mind, I could take it, all wrapped up in my fur. But Rex!

And at that the bear looked more sad than ever before they had seen her, so sad that it cut at every heartstring and the deer, shaking, got up and said might he be excused. The bear hardly heard him, so busy she was trying to hold back her own tears, so the sheep took it on herself to say: I won't let you! There's some things you've got to face! Whereupon he said he had already faced them and once was enough, and began to bawl shamelessly as the sheep tugged at him and the birds, so easily perturbed, began to chitter and the grey goose hissed at all of them to shut up and keep still.

The bear finally restored order by saying: Think of the giraffe! And the deer, always easily gulled, thought it meant this crisis too would work out for the best, and so consented to stay. And just to show he was a man, too.

Then the bear told the rest very quickly.

Rex had stumbled in his stall with all that pitching and tossing and wallowing in the wicked deep cradle of the waves and stumbled so badly that one fine little stem of a leg, oh one little beauty of a forefoot as slim as could be had been hurt at the kneecap. And the bear placed her paw on her knee as if it were her heart beating there.

I didn't know it, she said, till we reached the other side. I mean this side, and were let out of that darkness and off the thing into another wagon. Then I saw him and saw he was *lame*!

Because of the way she said *lame*, the lame-legged bird seemed to realize his own tragedy for the first time and uttered a shrill, Cock-Robin-killed cry. Oh my little chickadee, cried the bear, I am so sorry. Do come and sit on the deer's lowest antler so I can see you. And the poor thing, mollified, did, though when he had settled himself, stretched one wing along that left wooden leg so conspicuously that he looked twice as much like a half-wounded dancer. Suffice it to say, both deer and bird hunched tensely there as if they might bolt any second.

I thought of everything, the bear went on. Cambric tea, French mint tea in compresses, like what got my sore paw well, tansy and sheep's laurel, meadow rue and bird-foot violet, sassafras bark mixed with beeswax, even, she half-grimaced, my own bear's grease.

I recalled all the other herbs mother had taught me, rosemary and periwinkle, heartsease and dittany, alder and elderberry and leaves of the lily. Horsebalm. Everything! I knew I could brew them, and mix this with that, and rub in rose hips and myrtle and moss. I knew that with hickory and fennel and dock and true sorrel and Solomon's seal and the juice of the bluet, that with wakerobin and syrup of sycamore sapling and bloodwort and snail slime and miller moth dust, and bee sweat and tear-spurge, roasted with pollen, I could stir and sift and pound and cook up a mess that put on that sweet knee of his and put on and put on again and again and applied first with snow from the mountains and next with heat from some hot spring and next mild as milk after it's an hour from the cow's udder, would make the knee right and better than ever! I knew it, and was ready to travel to mountain and hot spring, and search all the river lands and every small woods and big woods and brook bottom and even seacoast for the dried weeds of it and treetops for the finest new leaves and roots of some fallen old oak, deep still in the ground, and blackberry tangle and swamps full of adders, and deserts even! I was ready to do all, and could have done it, quick as a wink, and saved him and saved him forever!

Well, but what was I in their eyes? We always have to think of that. What was I in their eyes? A mere bear. Did they listen to me? Did I have a chance to get out? I never saw such steel bars as they make here. So instead they called in a horse doctor who fiddled and fumed and ho-hummed and hee-hawed and said that Rex my darling, Rex who was Hansel, Rex the very genius of his kind, Rex, inspiration, Rex who could take an idea like that!—the bear clicked her claws—and translate it into the most ravishing little step—and she put one paw to her muzzle in the French manner—Rex more king than lion, was *finished*. And she slapped the armchair so hard with one paw that the bird who had been ostentatiously balancing on his wooden leg slipped and fell off the deer's antler.

Kind bear, carried away, did not even notice.

Finished, my darling, finished!

I nearly went mad. I couldn't believe it. I raved, I roared, I almost tore out those bars, I refused to eat, I lost my looks, my fur fell out in patches, I didn't care. I said: if he was finished so was I. I meant it. I never meant anything more.

And oh but—she put her paw to her eyes—if they had just let us talk. If during all those dark days I could have told him what I believed and knew in my heart, if I could have said to him, I know this recipe and I know that. If I could have repeated lore, all my bear's lore, and mother's too, and rhythm and rhyme and incantation. If I could have murmured old gypsies' words and magical phrases—if by anything during that time I could have kept his spirit and kept it flying, for he was a flying horse, my dears.

But no. I was in one big place with Bosco and countless zebras and camels, and other bears that I must say I hated, and other horses I couldn't endure to look at, let alone smell, and monkeys again and something they called a chimp, and lions. Name them all. All were there. And what did I care. While he, in constant conference, in confabulation, in consultation, was torn from my sight and never after that glimpse I had of him when I saw his hurt leg, did we meet! Think of it! Us, who had traveled together and made such an act, who were considered inseparable, and virtually twins, who had out of nothing, mere chance and god-witted intelligence, created something, and a quite incomparable something, too, that brought the house down and paved their way, *their way, not ours*, with gold, to think that at that moment we were parted, that one moment in history!

She panted with pain and fury.

I never forgave them. I never will. That thing they call a heart in their breasts—it's made of stone, it beats only for themselves, or gold. What do they care for us? We don't partake of the same world, they think. We are their inferiors, can be kicked and starved and employed—without union wages!—and trussed up in cages and made to slave—sixteen hours a day pulling our guts out—I'm thinking of horses—or trained to amuse them. They're fools, fools, fools!

All her fur in a wrath, she got up and paced the floor back and forth, while cat of green eyes devoured her, and the goose squawked sadly to herself, and the deer and the lame-legged bird bent their heads as if shattered. Only the sheep kept her presence of mind, looking cool and steadfast ahead of her.

When the bear's rage had subsided, she turned and said: I did make a scene now, didn't I? But forget it. It's only that the unjustness of it flares up and scalds me. But—*c'est la vie*. And she plumped down again.

The day for Madison Square Garden came. Need I add that Rex and I had been deceived here too. It wasn't a garden, no more than a woods is. No garden, just a name! Well, I went out there into it all. Not one ring but three, and perfectly huge, with sawdust colored green. Were the animals supposed to think they were walking on grass? I went through my act, alone. Remember that everything had happened very quickly, there was no time to schedule and train a new horse—and besides, *I* wouldn't have it. The new owner was furious. How he cursed me, and said nobody could think a lone bear tapping a drum at all funny. I didn't care. I played the piano, I shuffled a quite subtle and intricate Czardas, I somersaulted—something I'd practiced to keep grief down—I rolled my eyes and held my nose high and put on that shako and mimicked a drum majorette. But it wasn't funny. The *esprit* was gone. I knew it. I didn't care.

Don't ask me about the rest. All bad. I was transferred and sold and sold again and tried out with new horses, two of whom I clawed, and my status fell, from engagement to engagement, and finally I was with what they call a one-horse circus, a little family affair that tours the smallest towns and has two dogs and one clown who also waters the animals and takes down the tent, and two or three acrobats who double for everything else too.

Oddly enough, the audiences in those small towns liked me the most though what a bore I must have been! and whistled and stamped just like they did at the fairs in Austria when I was so young. But all pride, all heart was gone. I wanted just one thing now. I dreamed it, I ate it, I thought it, night and day. And that was liberty. And finally one day I got it. It was the trees on the mountains I saw, and the snow I thought would be there I might have stolen for Rex's knee. It was the trees and the snow on the mountain tops that did it. Inspired, I was inspired again, and with marvelous cunning bided my time just after the act—I waited, you see, for that—and then, play-acting at lunging, and falsettoing a roar, scared them all out of their wits, and was off.

And so I made my way, for the town was pressed up against the very side of the mountain, over boulders and streams, and up spurs and crests and through big woods and little, to here.

The deer, confused, said, you mean now?

And the bear had to explain no, it was then, and that was when the hotel got started.

And so you had us and the hotel, the goose remarked with rather squalid sentimentality, but the bear was too dog-tired to answer and besides, the raccoon chose that moment to wander in, followed by a friend he had just managed to make, a woodchuck, who carried a bouquet of red clover in one paw and who immediately upon sitting down reared up on his hind legs and proceeded to nibble one head of it as if it were a nut.

Showoff! the cat thought, and lifted his upper lip in a most ugly fashion. The rest of the animals didn't like it either, thinking it ill-mannered of one to eat when the others weren't eating, and especially rude of the raccoon to burst in like that when he had missed so much of the story already and nearly all wished that the bear would address some withering remark to the raccoon and especially his friend, who had not been invited!

But the bear looked positively muzzled, as if she might never speak again, and sunk in her fur, just sunk in it! So a long little silence reigned as the woodchuck polished off flower after flower. It makes one so nervous! complained the goose. The rest of the birds took time out for a snooze and even the deer, spent with so much vicarious suffering, closed his eyes.

But the cat, angered first by that presumptuous woodchuck, pulled at his paw with vexation. He felt most dissatisfied with reality as the bear had presented it. It did seem to him she had made a real blunder: she shouldn't have let that horse throw her the way he did but then, women were always too easily affected by everything and particularly by anything to do with love. It was all wrong, and he had always known it. Keep yourself to yourself—it had been his motto. If the bear had, she would still be the rage of the circus and leading a great life of greasepaint and hot lights, the toast of the town and the Queen

70

of the Garden instead of just having this hotel to run with a real tedious garden you had to weed. And really, he thought, were the animals truly interesting that she lived with after a fashion of speaking? Look at that raccoon and woodchuck! Look at the goose and the dove! My stars, look at the sheep and the deer. All of them either superannuated or just born boobies! Why, with the exception of himself—and heaven knew why he continued to stay on—nobody had any real charm or vitality or fascination!

The cat narrowed his eyes in a sly sneer. The bear had settled too easily for a domain of strictly inferiors. Easy enough to be the big cheese with dolts like the deer. Easy enough to be the focus of admiration for a lame-legged bird and a blind mole and a giddy chipmunk! Queen of the cast-offs, that's what she was, and it was time for him to be leaving! His tail was now lashing. Soon, he thought, it will hold me up when I walk on my back legs, and he stretched with the exuberance of ego, but the sheep plucked at him and said: Wait, you fool, there's more to it than this!

The cat knew at once what she meant. The horse! Not that dead one she'd been talking about, but the live one who had caused them such grief.

Yes, he mewed silently, what about him?

I'll see that we find out, answered the sheep grimly.

So the cat remained, sitting down on his haunches, erect as a robin or an Egyptian, while the sheep ruminated, shifting cud from left side of her mouth to the right, on just how the bear might be shaken out of her fur, enough, at least, to tell the *real* story, the one that mattered, as to where she had been and what had become of her and the horse.

The sheep thought she had it down pat: it hurt any mother more to lose her children than for a child to lose its mother. Sure the bear had had a bad experience years upon years upon years ago, but it stood to reason, considering the fact that your mother had to be older than you, that she was going to die first, and whether it happened sooner or later, it was all a matter of lawful necessity. But that was not true of one's children. If one's children were younger than oneself and one still lost them, then that was not a lawful necessity but an unlawful accident. And one had a *right* to suffer. Now, if she was going to feel sorry for anybody, it would be for the bear's mother who had had to see her cub torn from her the way she herself had had her own lambs torn from her. And the sheep coughed at the remembrance of emotion. Yeah but, she thought, getting over her spell, none of this applied to the horse. Why, the bear showed her true calibre there, and it was not too admirable, one had to admit! Growing so silly over someone like that! And raving and losing weight just because he got sick and left the act! Besides, she had admitted that life had its drawbacks and after all, the hotel was the thing. Where else could she have such devoted friends, who gave her rubdowns and brought her strawberries, kept the mice away, and charmed her with stories and musical evenings? Why, speaking for herself, she'd spit on a life like that, showing off for a bunch of kidnappers, whiskers and boots and all, who'd rip the skin off your back if they had half a chance, and eat your own children before your eyes!

Besides, she thought crossly, wasn't the bear rather putting it on? All that talk about lotions and potions and going to the mountains for snow! What made her think she was such a good doctor, better than a real qualified horse doctor, and what made her think just *talking* might cure him, and she wondered, she did, if the horse was *really* that good or pretty or loving. Who knows, he might have deliberately hurt his knee, just to get away from the bear! After all, hadn't she said he was getting tired of it all, working so hard six days out of seven? And what future was in it? Glory one day and ashes the next! Because, don't try to tell her they kept you on when you got older or old. Out on the dustheap for you, my fine fellows! Out indeed! Whereas for her, and all the ones here, why they depended on nobody's say, not even the bear's—was this hotel so necessary? —not at all! Think of all the animals who managed very well without it, and when they got old they got old and no questions asked and in the meantime they worked for nobody and life was secure. All that glory business, and all that love too, what was more treacherous? The higher you went the more of a fall you were bound to have! Stick to the middle course! that was her rule, stay where you belonged, in the rut and the groove. Nothing turned upside down then, and you didn't go berserk either!

The sheep returned to that point again. It did seem to her, yes it did, that the bear had just lost control of herself, and probably became a nuisance, too, to that horse. Nobody should do that. It wasn't seemly. Excess was always in bad taste. Tut, tut! And she clicked her tongue against that warm comforting cud. Or—her yellow eyes went very hard—was there another ruse behind it all? Was she just putting it on? Was she just trying to wind them up in her story so that they would think better of the *real* horse, and be ready to forgive him and the bear too? Be ready to receive him with open arms when in a few days he quietly made his appearance? It'd be like the bear to have him planted on the next hill, awaiting further instructions. The sheep could see the bear clambering that shaky stairway to wave a white scarf from the top of it and the horse at his outpost tearing down through the woods, drunk on the go-ahead signal! And in he would come, to be courted and fêted, and given the deer's chamber no doubt—oh she went hot with rage at that—and if anyone cheeped, out they'd go too, my fine woolly, feathered or antlered ones, out they'd go, for here's the real kingpin come home at last!

73

With the hotel gone to pot in six weeks! Hadn't it been proved already? Why, with him here he'd have Tom, Dick and Harry in for supper, with a mare soon, no doubt—good enough for the bear!—and little ones growing up, and all their first person singular life, all their nice bachelor camaraderie gone to grass.

The sheep nearly swallowed her cud at that, and had to clear her throat several times. When she did, she took the plunge.

Well bear, she started off, that was a wonderful story but we still don't know where you've been all these days, do we? And she turned to the other beasts for support.

The sheep said this so snappily, with such a crack of a challenge in each blattered syllable, that the bear, in spite of that heavy dream she seemed to have been slumbering in, was roused up. Just the same, she hadn't heard properly, and the sheep had to repeat her devastating remark.

Oh! said the bear at that, oh! But she was finding it hard to place herself and led off with some remark about how it hadn't been days she was away but year, years, my dears!

We happen to know, replied the sheep sourly, that it was just *days*.

The bear wagged her head and said she was only being allegorical.

The sheep looked as if she were about to butt and let forth triumphantly, all her suspicions come home to roost: You mean you were just making all that up?

Oh indeed no, replied the bear, gathered together at last. All that was more true than truth, my friend. I was only saying, and in a manner of speaking, that the days when I was away from you seemed like centuries.

The deer nearly swooned at this turn of phrase and the dove bowed frantically, while all the birds chippered deliciously, but the sheep wasn't being taken in, no siree!

74

All right, she blatted, suppose it was an eternity to us too?

You don't know how we felt, put in the cat, touched in spite of himself and irked at the sheep's blatant matter-of-factness.

But what I want to know, the sheep pushed on brutally, was just where were you? Shouldn't we know that?

The bear, looking rather hurt at this matronly baiting, said with grand dignity: Why, I had every intention of telling you but it does seem to me rather late for such a long story this evening.

No, no! they all cried. No, no! A chorus of cries went up to the welkin. Oh please, dear bear! whimpered the deer and three birds swooped down with daring precision, and the cat to beg her rolled on his back most voluptuously. Nor did they let up, they kept crying please, and do go on, and we can't sleep unless we know, and what does it matter if it is late, do we *have* to get up in the morning, and, finally, we'll just die if you don't!

The bear had been shaking her head all the time but when they shouted: We'll just die! and the birds swung around like a merry-go-round and the deer hopped on three legs and then capered and the cat, practicing back-leg walking, staggered at last against her knees, she had to laugh and call them her naughty ones which indeed they all felt to be, even the sheep who, suddenly caught up in the general ardor, baaed as tremulously as a young lamb.

So the animals won—they nearly always did—and though the bear was exhausted, she motioned them to get back to their places and settle down. But please bear, begged the chipmunk, mayn't I sit on your lap? Well, the bear said, since it was the last lap, he might, whereon the animals had to laugh though jealousy was at once afire in them and the cat thought: I'll give it to that chip later. Even the deer felt it wasn't fair of the chipmunk to take advantage that way when all the rest had forborne. What if he was the smallest! But the bear who rarely, if ever, showed favorites, seemed to need to do so right then. Had she sensed the disloyalty of the cat? In any case, the sheep's attitude had come through very clearly. So she let the chipmunk nestle right on her chest and stroked him all through the recital with a maddening regularity—and with such a sensuous fondness, yearned all the animals.

WHAT everyone knew was that it had to start off with the horse, and the bear didn't disappoint them. Yes, the horse, only she called him the colt. I suppose, she confessed, you didn't like him. In fact, it was hard to overlook. You're not very subtle, she smiled at the sheep. Which is all to the good in a hotel like this. I believe in democracy. I believe that the will of the majority has to prevail. In a cooperative like this, which you *might* call it, if it doesn't it becomes tyranny. And we can't have that. But just the same, since I was, in a way, running this place, I thought I had *some* rights. I knew it would not be acceptable to have him stay here. I never dreamed of it. Never even entertained the notion. You understand that, I hope. Since she stopped at this direct appeal the animals all, if belatedly, nodded their heads.

But do you see—the bear turned her muzzle up, a most warm and tender light settling in the blue eye—I liked him so, and he needed something. He needed something so much. And I'll frankly tell you that I was torn, torn between my clear recognition of my duty, my democratic duty, and those private instincts of my heart. But this is always the way it goes, my dears. Everybody who is anybody knows what is just and right, but it's another thing to do it. It's one thing to have a nice compact and unified harmonious little society, and it's another thing to deal with the charming outsider, who always will come in!

So I did know something of all your dissatisfaction! My dear cat, I saw you didn't pay your rent! But I thought—do you know what I thought? I thought: just give me time, it's time that I need . . . With time it will all work out. So I tried to balance as best I could, and I don't say I did very well. Sometimes when things are like that one's only recourse is to ignore, is just to pretend you don't see half of it, because otherwise one would be too hopelessly distracted by all the demands of statesmanship. I thought to myself about those mice: I know they're bad for the deer, and bad for the morale, and bad for housekeeping . . . just as I knew it was bad of you, cat, not to catch them! Coquettishly she waved a paw at him. But I also figured: they can't in a few days bring the hotel down and the deer can sleep outside if he must, and eventually I will straighten it all out and show those little rats their places. So that's how it went. Of course I wasn't figuring on all this extra time, I mean the time when I disappeared, and what was my first thought when I started making tracks for home, or rather, my second thought, for the first and the last was of you, my dears, why, it was of those mice and what would have happened—would they have gnawed the foundations? How I wished we had made them gnaw-proof!

Well, anyhow, about all that . . . I said the colt needed me, and he did. You see, he had run away. It was the old thing. He had been born on a farm and it wasn't the place for him and he had the sense to recognize it first off. I respected him for that more than I can say. I've seen so many animals trying to adjust, to accept their lot, to be resigned patiently to a life of small pleasure or no pleasure at all, all duty, all hay and no oats, that whoever strikes out and kicks at the traces—well, my hat's off to him. So it was with this colt.

And then besides, she said with a look of pain, he was spotted. Not like Rex was. Oh not by half. But still, he was. And he did have nice feet, not like Rex's, but still they were nice, and could be quite good in time, I knew. Well, he took to me and I don't know why, any more than I ever knew why Rex did, but he did, and saw through that scolding I gave him in the birch grove, and wouldn't take no for an answer, and was somehow so clever about it all, and really beguiling in a way no horse has been since Rex. Oh how I had come to hate them, you know, after Rex was taken away!

But this fellow. . . . Not that he was the spitting image of Rex, or not that I thought he was *Rex Redivivus*, or any such nonsense, for I'm *not* a fool, but he *did* please me, and there was a sense about him of undeveloped talent that did go straight to my heart. I didn't believe the world was just waiting for him the way I believed it with Rex—and don't say it's age that makes the difference—for with Rex I was right, the world was waiting, that horse has already gone down in history and me, I'm proud to say, along with him. Consult any annals of the circus!

Even the sheep gasped at that, while the rest of the animals simply looked cockeyed.

But I did think, the bear went on, as if she hadn't made such a staggering claim, that he had something in him, which I alone could help him find.

Now at first I didn't think of the circus, one speck. I was finished with that, it was the half of my other life dead and buried. This was during the time that I was treading time, like you do when you're treading water, and just waiting to see what would come out of it. I met him, I will admit, and heard out his troubles. He didn't have many because he was so young, but whatever they were they added up to one thing: that he had run away and he was ready to run farther, and he wanted a fine good life out of it.

He had heard something of racing and seemed to have his heart set on that after I told him what a footsore life it would be to draw hansom cabs in New York City. Now I had seen enough horses run round a ring in Madison Square Garden so

79

I said: run for me, and he ran. I studied his gait. He had an early foot all right, and his legs did slam out when he was on the home run in an efficient and even thrilling fashion, but I wondered, just looking at him and his build if he really had it in him for that gruelling trade. And anyhow, a race course would be miles away, and I had no idea where nor had the colt, and it feared me to think of him setting out over mountains and hillsides and through all our forests to make the big trek down. I thought of all that we know, my dears, she observed sombrely.

The deer thought: I might have pierced him with one of my antlers and the sheep thought; I'd have laid wait and butted him northwest, and the cat thought of himself and the bobcat pouncing down from a tree branch onto that satin back, and everybody grew very proud over the amazing powers they possessed.

Well, I dillied and dallied and shillied and shallied, trying to keep him, all the while, from coming right out and asking me if he too could stay here and live with us all. For I say *this* about him also. He wanted adventure and a gallant life but the other thing, our *gemütlich* thing, appealed to him more than it should have at his age, and it was this that especially decided me against his seeking a racetrack tout and joining up with all that. Believe me, I was almost at my wit's end when along he came one day, having made a big sortie out into the unknown—something I very much encouraged him in—to say that he'd seen an assortment of animals riding along in a wagon on some road that led into some town . . . and what did I think that was? I well knew. It was some little circus, of course, I said, and explained very cautiously what I meant, but the sawdust was already in his nostrils . . . and he leapt at once to the idea that this was what he'd been waiting for.

One is thoughtless, gets carried away, and I could have bit my tongue out for having said *circus*, but still, did *you* want him here? And was I just to send him packing, without advice or training, or anything, to be caught by his master or lost in the mountains or stung by a snake? So his will prevailed. I grudgingly told him just something of what I knew—I will say that for him I kept my career strictly in *this* country—and he was filled with adoration and said I must teach him all I knew. I said, boy, if you could learn that, you'd be head of the country! Anyhow, it did begin. One two, one two . . . I beat out the rhythms and showed him the steps. How it all came back! I'd forgot nothing and the colt was fired and learned just a third as fast as Rex but still he learned and I saw that sure enough there was the makings of a nice firehouse pony doing his stuff well enough for a one-horse circus. So the weeks went by and the mice multiplied while that colt mastered first positions and some rather nice extensions and got so he could stay on his hind legs for three minutes though never could he manage to dance on them, and had, as he thought, the naive one, a little act all cooked and roasted to a very turn. I knew better and told him so.

I said did he know what practice it took if you didn't have genius? He said, but I have, and when the audience is there I'll be twice as good. I said, alas my dear, they're most unforgiving and very capricious, and harder to please than a bear with a sore head, and no sooner do you master one trick than they want ten better ones, and so chattered on of life as I knew it. But it's always the same thing, if young ones could learn from their elders, we'd really have progress. Advice was nothing, warning less. The amateur's usual attitude, she added, staring at the cat's tail and the hair on his spine, all of it rising from some hidden emotion.

But since time was of the essence and I knew that soon he would be staying here, unable to tear himself away from my motherly interest, storming and pleading, unless I said: here's your diploma, now get! I went on with it, and taught him and taught him, and finally managed to beat a lot into that vain skull of his. I will say he got so he worked, and would practice when I wasn't there to hound him, and began to show towards the last some independence of an artistic attitude, and to reveal a modicum of taste, at least, about the angles of the forefoot, and the turn of the neck, and so on. But vain! He was vain in a frivolous way, not like Rex who was superbly vain, in a majestic and justified way. So he wanted me to braid his mane, which *was* long and silky, with a red ribbon like he had seen done on the farm, and wouldn't let me rest till I had, though I told him real horses despised such frippery. When it was done, how he preened himself. I told him all he needed was a brook to look into and he'd fall in love with himself and he said no, he'd hold it up to me, and I said, oh la la, those days are over. Well, with all this horse play he was beside himself, and wove little steps around me to make me a prisoner. That's how we were going on out there by that big turfy field. The colt had run here in times past though I knew it was a dangerous place. We favored a little grove mostly. But he liked the field because it was open though I'd said that just because it was, it exposed him and me to a lot we had both been avoiding.

So I got him back into a shaded section and said, Now boy of the beautiful ribbon, go through your paces from A to Z. I'm the audience and I'm tired and bored, and I'm waiting to be shown. Very little will please me, I've seen it all and even if I haven't I wouldn't know, I'm voracious, I'm predacious, and my only asset is that I'm also simple-minded. Gull me and I will be hooked. Throw the sand of charm in my eyes and I'll writhe on the seats.

The bear stared at the cat's swollen tail once more. That's how I had to be with him—stern and tough.

So he started off. It was what you might call one of our last rehearsals for time was getting on. If he wanted to land in that circus it wouldn't be there forever and by the end of the summer all would be up and, besides, the mice would have turned us out!

He did very well that day, set up by the red ribbon no doubt. Did very well, forgot next to nothing, maintained a consistency of style, clicked his hooves like an officer, and stirred by my words on Rex, perhaps, was as charming as a bumpkin can be. I was absorbed, I will say, beating time for one thing, and watching each turn so I'd have all my points ready at hand when it came time to criticize, and pleased, too, by his unexpected favors of grace. Maybe, I was thinking, this colt does have something . . . when lo and behold, I was jerked back in the most indescribably painful way, jerked off my log, with my arms pinned to my sides, right onto some outcrop of a rock. What a crack on the head it gave me, and next thing I knew, a chain was around my back legs and two fellows, as swarthy as my first gypsies, were at me looking scared and mean and hurting me fearfully, and the colt had been lassoed too, with a great rope. He whinnied, I bellowed, but who was to hear us, let alone save us? We put up a grand fight but of course they didn't play fair—when do they ever?—and eventually we were both of us thrown in a wagon and hauled away. It was the old days over again! I fell into a stupor, into jungle fever and a pitfall of melancholia, and it's just possible lost my reason for some little while, thinking that he was Rex and I myself of former days and we were going from Prague to Paris or Lyons to Arles. I didn't know which, I couldn't tell where, delirium surely seized me and held me more captive than those gypsies for days on days.

Well, it was a flip-flop of fate and a back-handed somersault at that. For if those dark shabby strong-smelling fellows didn't belong to the circus and if it wasn't the one-horse one that the colt had described! I thanked my stars it wasn't the other one, that I had run from, but I was fearful my fame might have spread even to this benighted one, and played as dumb as I could and as awkward, and growled so much I got a sore throat! But then it occurred to me after the first days of protest and the nightmare of it swooping down over me that it was worse to be in the cage where they could taunt me and poke at me with sharp sticks than out of it where, on my feet, I could take a swat at them if I had to, and regain also my sense of fitness. So, becoming conciliatory, I showed I did have some brains and, more than that, overwhelmed them when ten minutes after they'd led me forth oh so gingerly on a chain, I began to make my mazurka. How those keeper gypsies jabbered! Oh mother tongue of my youth! I heard all the old words dashed in—what a paprika of Vienna and Budapest and Dresden and Munich, and quick did they call the family of jugglers that owned the show, and so I strutted my stuff again, and the colt—who had been separated from me, as usual—saw it where he was tethered to a post and reared up on his hind legs exuberantly and then lowering himself began to go through his own little paces. Everybody was flabbergasted and the owners shook hands with the keepers and the woman almost kissed me.

I must say, I was pleased with the colt. Poor fellow, I learned sometime later that he had had absolute stage fright when he did set foot in his dream place and hadn't done anything, nothing at all, but crop at the sawdust and try to kick if somebody came near. And the shock of it too had upset him. He'd had dreams of walking there, and gallantly offering his talents for a certain commission of fame and good feeding. But to be kidnapped instead, so uncouthly and roughly, had knocked all his notions into a cocked hat . . . so gently is youth brought up these days. The bear smiled. So I did that much for him, I did!

We went on that night, separately, since how could I tell

them there could be an act? But the show was so mingy and unprofessional with such a fat pony carrying such a fat woman, and such feeble dogs going through such low-held hoops that I saw the two of us could take it over. And believe me, by the end of the first evening I was ready to introduce our act, in spite of my better wisdom, and did, and the others saw it and howled with glee and the next evening when we went through it, there was such an intaking of breaths and such an adorable silence, that kind you can split a horsehair with, that I knew it could be all mine again. All mine. All that old world again. They were eating out of our hands and the colt he was eating out of mine too.

True enough, he would never match Rex, but true enough too, he did fizz up with an audience there, he was the vain kind who had to have hand claps, he didn't love it for the sheer love of it which is what the great ones do. Why, Rex would dance in a blind alley and be as happy with only mice watching as with crowned heads in London. But what of that? A second-string fellow is better than a third-string one, and for those not in the know virtually first-string. We proved it by the audiences we got. The circus had been ready to move on. Did it? It stayed and stayed, with every bench full every night. All those hayseeds splitting their sides at us and the children in very hysterics.

I was in a dream, I forgot the mice though none of you, my dears. Oh I did think of you! and wondered how was the barley field coming along and would the raccoon keep off the otter, and how was the beebalm the weeds love so, and thought of what you'd be eating. I did worry about that. But this life, this life, you know. It did hold me, it did. A dream, that's all, a dream! And the colt was so pleased, and that pleased me, and so ready to work for the incentive of hand claps and so nice to me that I almost thought: he deserves it for me to stay on, it's right for me to give him this break, and suppose the circus

85

doesn't have its old lure, wouldn't mother have done it, there are sacrifices one ought to make. . . .

But then I thought of all of you too and thought, though perhaps I'm only mistaken—she showed her teeth gaily—that you needed me too, though not any sacrifice, and altogether I was between no and yes and one bundle of hay and another. And it was the same as before, when I first met the colt, a dream came down over me. I knew I would have to decide soon but I knew I couldn't as yet, and so I let things take their course and drifted with the stream.

We went to another town and set up shop there and it was more of the same with the colt in his clover and me with my own lion's share. But I told him too that it was a one-horse circus and far beneath our respective talents. I had to inform him of status, you know, otherwise the chap would have thought it was Sells Floto, with all Europe in the bag. Well, when he heard this, he said let's get on to better ones, and that was when I began to think. Better ones! I'd had the best! Must I begin that old climb again, that tedious, that banal climb to the top? Let it be for the colt, let him struggle up, let him get winded and spavined and sway-backed and shorn of illusions and shredded of hope but, intact and all whole in his skin, *arrive there*. I had. Yes, and nothing would have stopped me, not even, I must own up, my own mother. But I had done it and I had had it, and the best had been. I had had the great dream and the king of horses, king's crowns might have glistened in some box, violets at least had blossomed on bosoms when I danced, and furs and velvet had come to applaud me, dancers had maybe learned a trick from Rex and clowns several turns from me, we had been the darlings of one world and that ought to be enough for any one bear.

I saw it all with a sudden most vivid clearness. Saw my youth come and pirouette, saw it twirl and whirl, as if in a magic glass, and whirl and bow and disappear. Saw there was no use trying to fly after it, no use trusting this new dream that was but an echo of the first profound dream, saw, and was content. Even when a prancing ghost came round, capering in caracoles, whirling in girandoles, even when he made mad figure-eights, and leapt in air, girdled in roses, a horseshoe of them, saw it was no use leaping after him. Rex was gone, and who knows where? Gone, and I hope to liberty! Gone and I hope to the wildwoods, gone, but I trust not where the woodbine twineth. Let Rex be immortal, like all ghosts are! That's what I said. Free, my darling, and dancing forever, dancing for mice to watch, if need be, and are mice so much less than men? Not in our world, where equality reigns, and each to his niche and opportunity for all!

The bear gasped, all but out of breath, and fighting again against some upheaval, while the animals still on tenterhooks thought: don't let her sink down into her fur! Especially the sheep thought this who, almost convinced of the bear's sincerity, was still impatient with so much emotion and deeply distrustful of its relevancy. Was it going to turn any water for them except tear-water? On with the facts! And her yellow eyes flashed: facts! facts!

But the bear had her own sense of story and was as eager to get on with it, and drive to the conclusion as anyone. It was simply that there was so much to tell, so much of her own heart to pour out. Not that the animals wanted it, but how could you tell a story without pouring it out? And to tell meant to tell all, to reproduce the attendant fevers, to try to capture the power of passion that drove you as a windmill drives water. Facts, facts—she clicked her claws. What were they? To deliver a fact would take one second. But the aura, the condition of feeling, the one thousand imperceptible shades of bloom and illusion that drove one here and drove one there! And otherwise, just to understand! How was she to reveal what she had undergone unless she herself ventured into the thick of it, into the complex of present emotions and past ones, and former notions and continuous ones, and textures of an old day and mixtures of today and endless days that experience was? Or sauntered for a while by headlong streams and brooks that took a side course but inevitably and despite their round-aboutness, returned to the main and single theme?

She got respite and breath and went on.

Such is our weakness, she began. Such is our essential, primeval folly, that who knows if I wouldn't have followed that colt and yielded to him for his own ambition, and linked my fate with his as though I were a first, a very young bear, with never a figment of a past behind me, who knows, had not chance played good cards again and caused me to make my own somersault. We are dilatory, we bears, dilatory and slow by nature, and hate to make up our minds, and dread the severing consequences of action, and with our will sunk into our fat, prefer and generally always, to go with the wind, where the bees lead us. And I might have. In spite of my thoughts of you, my dears, and the hotel and my proud propertied claims, I might have stayed on for the sake of the colt and entered again that sweated captivity to line somebody else's pockets, might have.

But there were bidders come. Big thick men from another circus who smoked cigarettes this time. They had heard of the colt and me. They wanted us. It was the first step up. All the rest would follow. When the colt heard of it he went wild. I just stood still, stiffening in my fur. You want to go, I said. *Do I?* he answered. Not me, I replied, for I saw what I knew and knew what I had to do and threw up the cards, every one, all the trumps of them and the trumpets, the trumpery too, and the triumphs. Not me, I repeated. I'm going. Oh he pleaded, he argued, he got down on his knees, he wept and he bowed. But I knew at last. How can I do without you, he cried, all his mane shaken and wild. You will do very well, I prophesied. And told him, sweet colt, he'd miss me, as didn't he think I'd miss him, and at first it'd be just a killjoy dark, day after day no more than the other, with the something missing you couldn't dare name, and the load of it heavy, all the dead heart. But that then there would come a day, and another, and finally the red-letter day when he'd know again that the world was his oyster though I'd not be there to sample it with him. And that was the day to count on, none other, and that was the day to work for. For sure as the sun comes up it would come, with the hand claps pounding under the big top, and better drums beating than mine ever did for the fanfare to follow.

Oh he cried and he cried and tossed his head wild but I knew he was taking to my world's experience, knew it curried favor and twitched at an early foot.

When that was done, I prepared myself. The bidders stood round watching us. They said we weren't bad, it meant we were damned good, but how such words had lost all their weight with me! I soon saw the deal had been concluded. We were to join up with their circus and naturally it was bigger and better.

Look colt, I said, for I had to be honest. Look dear, I've had it, you know. Oh bear, bear! he began. I hushed him. I'm leaving, I said. After our act. I know how to do it, and it can be done. Later it'll be twice as hard. So it's now or never. Listen! I said, snatching at my last folly, you can come too if you want to, and stay at the hotel. We'll make arrangements somehow. You can come, you know, but *do you want to*? How he quivered at that! Oh colt, I said, it wouldn't be right. Your life is before you! You can get there—get where I got! It's in the stars and the cards! Go on with it, go on with this offer, outdo yourself, and get to another, and so travel up and up, all the rungs, and when you arrive there, think of me! Think of me who was once there too, and think of what it all means and be glad, and know it was worth it, but have a nice thought for old bear, too, who had to leave when she did!

Never did I see such profuse grief mixed as it was with gratitude and an odd, slinking remorse, and regret, and ambition. He wanted it all, that great life, though I fear he might never get it quite . . . But what could I do but encourage him, and fire him with want and spur him with will to be a very soldier in the whole hopeless task? I maybe did wrong, I don't know, but it had to be glory, glory, glory, a flaunting of banners and pennants and music and timbrels and ecstasy, or I myself would have just collapsed. For I saw I loved him too, in my own after way, in my way after Rex, and was giving up something—no longer the false lights and the tinsel shine, but a new thing filled with a congeries of hazards.

But I did.

I waited. The first night was no good. Nor the second. By then I was fit to be tied, for the transfer was about to take place. It was our last night in that town and with that circus. After our acts, with the usual thunder of applause, I stood shaking. I whispered to the colt my last words and then with stupendous effort I flung myself from my keeper, snapped my chain, and having consulted all canvas exits, was off through the nearest one.

Passion and fury gave me wings. I ran as never have I run. Suffice it to say, I made it, vaulted up to the first hill, and lost in a bramble that tore my skin, knew I was safe. Torches and searchlights played for a while, but were soon extinguished. I heard the colt whinny after me like in a sweet wish to follow after and take up too, the good way of the life in my hotel. But at last I could hear him no longer and I was alone to trundle my way disheveled and weary, over brooks and through swamps, up hills and down, following my nose. . . . It was a grand trip, my dears. Miles and miles of it! I can't tell you how much of my fur will furbish birds' nests next year. But life is like that. And now I'm back. And glad to be. So glad, so glad.

And the bear, at that, clasping the chipmunk to her, in such a hug that she almost extinguished him, at last let him go and fell, tongue out, into tears, and tears, and sleep, while the animals tiptoed away, each to his own proper bed. . . .

So the bear slept very late the next morning as all the animals did and day followed day as it ever had, from more strawberry fêtes to cherry fiestas with fish fries and berry-picking parties, apple hunts and pear pluckings and nutting in fall for the chipmunk. No more rooms got builded and the correspondence somewhat died down though the bear had her applications she must ponder on. Eventually and in the future, as she dreamed it, others would be allowed to come in but all that depended on everything else, and for the present she was content to file away the most promising letters and discard all the rest.

She wore her thick collar until her wound healed, and it did give her a smart appearance since it encouraged the fur to stand up around it like an Elizabethan ruff. But too soon it reminded the bear of what she would best not remember. A firm character that way, she liked chapters closed once they had been thoroughly opened. So she asked the raccoon, since the beaver was still so busy, if he might bring his friend the woodchuck around to bite through the leather with his sharp teeth. The raccoon obliged and the woodchuck spent a most pleasant afternoon on the bear's shoulder and next her hot heart, gnawing away at the collar with his quick little teeth. If the woodchuck took some time longer than was strictly necessary it was because, as he told the raccoon later, that he felt the bear to be almost an aunt—their coats, for one thing, were so thickly similar, and something, too, in the shape of their bodies! The raccoon, as usual, remained silent but privately determined to steer his friend clear of what he thought to himself by now was no more than a bear trap. Everybody so damned fond of her and that hotel!

As for the sheep, the bear had given her a passionate longing to tell her own story. She pictured it to herself over and over, the animals gathered around with the bear in the center but herself in the bear's big chair. . . and first that account of her own mother who was as good as the bear's mother, any day, and next the barnyard which, after all, had almost as many animals as a circus had and just as interesting and far more useful . . . why she herself personally happened to find it dull to hear about that giraffe and Bosco and did the bear really know what a farm was like? She'd tell her all right, she'd do it up brown, with all of it leading up to the day . . . oh that day, oh when her lambs came . . . such sweetness, such whiteness, such woolly things, and the first time they tottered all wobbly and weak and their first little baas—why when she looked in their eyes, what pretty little eyes they had, and the cosiness of it until—until! . . . What a story it would be, what a story! She'd wring the tears from them, that was one thing sure, why the deer would be all of a heap in two seconds, and the goose. . . .

For after all, the sheep thought triumphantly, I've been something the bear never was . . . a mother!

She baaed softly to herself. And if the bear had been, if she had, would she have been so silly over that horse? I'll say not, she thought, picturing her perfect, her precious lambs, you bet not, she baaed again.

As for the cat, he had acquired a distaste for *Eng-ish* though he couldn't say why. In any case, the ambition to learn it or talk with the bear about it had had its own little death. But not the other! He practiced on hind legs daily and made of the grey goose a confidante, going into the theory of balance by two legs as opposed to four, till the creature who had no other knowledge than what her feet gave her became very bewildered and as a recourse talked more about flying than walking.

Flying, of course, was in the cat's line too, for he had not dismissed the trapeze—by no means! and with birch bough and grapevine did marvelous things, hooking by tail and forepaw up and up till he encountered very clouds almost. The only thing was, he did it alone with merely a catbird to see and jeer. It grew harder, having no audience, it took moral energy to practice and practice and he thought of Rex's rewards and the bear's and even that colt's. Soon the thought spoiled his pleasure, he began to fret, and took to wandering about in a deep introversion or with a bored air would go out of the hotel and in again and out again and finn again . . . The bear, watchful once more, asked him one day was he off his feed? And the cat, bursting out with the dread secret of his ambition, told all. How she laughed. Why, they couldn't see you for fleas. Unless you want to join a flea circus.

The cat was incensed and outraged until the bear, taking him on her knee, tried to explain about magnitude, density and dimension. But he stuck to his point. If dogs could . . . Dogs aren't as little and low as you, she chaffered. The cat was beside himself, for she would not save his ego until she, turning very sobersides, said: If I'd have known that story was going to turn your head. . . . Why didn't I keep my big mouth shut, hurrying on to say that even trick dogs had had their day in the circus except for the one-horse kind she had described, and as for *cats*—what did he think lions were? And seeing his sad sulky profile, told him he looked just like a weathered old lion himself, only on another scale, and sketched in his heritage.

It took some while to convince the cat that he truly was so grandly connected, but at last he believed, and it did give him pleasure as he stalked in thickets.

But not really for long. So far as the cat was concerned, the bear really should have kept her big mouth shut. Life never was quite the same thing again and in dreams he perpetually flew over faces, mistaking the thunder of his own heart for thunderous applause.

But as for the rest, that story died out sweetly. First near at hand, like a painted stage scenery, it moved farther away with each day. On the first hill the first week, in the first forests the second week, it was soon where it should be, at the turfy field on that other side by the thin young forest, that side to which they would never cross. So it remained there, a rich old background, acquiring with season on season the patinas of gilt fading and lichen lodging and rain dimming and snow clinging and moss covering.

The bear was of it. It lurked just that much, and at seconds a gesture would call up a horse dancing and a bear in a thick collar with apron and cap, tapping a drum. But, like the smoke from an old caravan traveling farther and farther into the hills, even that little haunting which troubled them too ceased in good time.

And the good times went on and on and on. Would they not go on, and forever?

DESIGNED BY EDITH MCKEON. SET IN MONOTYPE
BEMBO AND PRINTED ON CURTIS UTOPIAN BY
THE STINEHOUR PRESS, LUNENBURG, VERMONT.
BOUND BY RUSSELL-RUTTER, NEW YORK CITY.